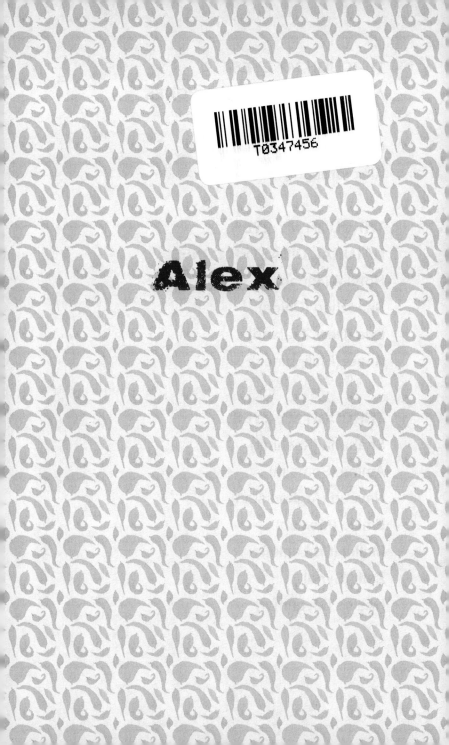

Alex

THROUGH MY EYES
AUSTRALIAN DISASTER ZONES
Tyenna (bushfire)
Mia (cyclone)
Alex (drought)

THROUGH MY EYES
NATURAL DISASTER ZONES
Hotaka (Japan)
Shaozhen (China)
Lyla (New Zealand)
Angel (Philippines)

THROUGH MY EYES
Shahana (Kashmir)
Amina (Somalia)
Naveed (Afghanistan)
Emilio (Mexico)
Malini (Sri Lanka)
Zafir (Syria)
Hasina (Myanmar)

THROUGH MY EYES AUSTRALIAN DISASTER ZONES

series editor Lyn White

ROSANNE HAWKE

ALLEN&UNWIN

SYDNEY · MELBOURNE · AUCKLAND · LONDON

First published by Allen & Unwin in 2023

Allen & Unwin
Cammeraygal Country
83 Alexander Street
Crows Nest NSW 2065
Australia
Phone: (61 2) 8425 0100
Email: info@allenandunwin.com
Web: www.allenandunwin.com

*Allen & Unwin acknowledges the Traditional Owners of the Country
on which we live and work. We pay our respects to all Aboriginal and
Torres Strait Islander Elders, past and present.*

A catalogue record for this
book is available from the
National Library of Australia

NATIONAL
LIBRARY
OF AUSTRALIA

ISBN 978 1 76087 700 2

Cover and text design by Sandra Nobes
Cover photos: Andrew McInnes / Austockphoto (boy); Bits and Splits /
Shutterstock (cracked earth); chris24 / Alamy (dust storm)
Map design by Guy Holt
Set in 11/15 pt Plantin by Midland Typesetters, Australia
This book was printed in July 2023 by the Opus Group, Australia.

10 9 8 7 6 5 4 3 2 1

For Richard and Elspeth

This story takes place in the Flinders Ranges region of South Australia. We acknowledge the traditional owners of this land, the Adnyamathanha people, who belong to the oldest continuing culture in the world and who cared for and protected Country for thousands of years. We honour and pay our respects to their elders, past and present.

The novel is set during 2020. The characters and some of the locations are fictional, to protect the privacy of communities and individuals. We have also altered some details and the chronology of various events, for the sake of the story, but the essential truths of the devastation caused by the drought remain.

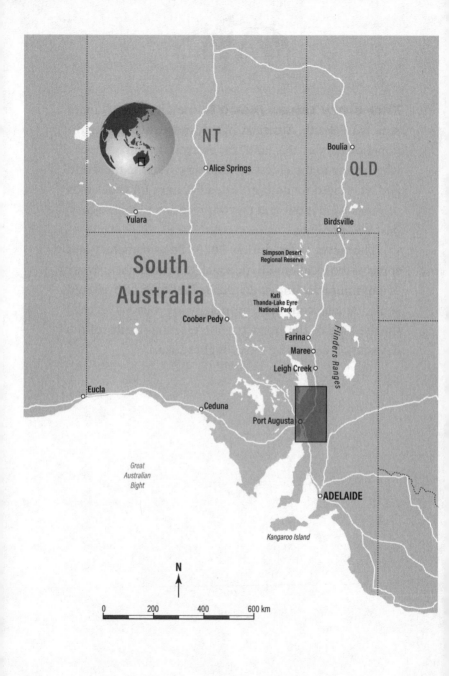

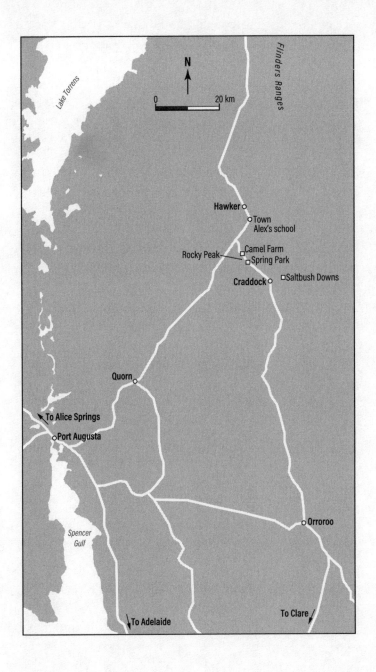

One

|||||||||||||||||||||||||||||||||||||||||||||||||||||||||||||||||||||||||||||||||

Alex Bray jumps off the school bus and gives a thumbs up to his mate Harry, the last kid still on board. At fifty-five kilometres, the bus run is a long trip – it feels especially long in the morning. Alex doesn't mind too much, though; it's the price of staying on Spring Park, the family's property. Tangi bounds up to meet him.

'You been waiting for me, girl?' He drops his bag and roughs up her black fur, then smooths the perfect tan triangles above her eyes. 'You love that, don't you, girl? So you missed me?' She barks once. 'Guess you're hoping I'll ride Jago.' That's when Tangi gets her best workout. Especially if she hasn't been helping Alex's mum with the sheep.

'What have you done all day?' he asks her. She yips, and Alex fills in the blanks as they walk the kay to the house. 'Cheered Dad up? You didn't rouse up my chickens, did you?' She looks at Alex as though she's saying, *As if.* 'You're impressive, Tangi.' The kelpie grins as she pads carefully beside him. 'I'm proud of you, girl.' She's so intelligent she's won muster dog trials.

The track winds through cracked brown paddocks until Alex's house comes into view. It's a colonial Aussie with a veranda all the way around, the tin roof designed to reflect the sun. The windmill cranks in the breeze, pumping water from the bore into the tank out the back. There used to be a rose garden in the front, and even a small patch of buffalo lawn, but now it's all as dried up as the paddocks.

He can see his dad sitting on the veranda. Will he say hello or not?

'Is that you, Alex?' Dad's watching the sky. He's always checking for clouds, or any sign that the weather will change. Farmers do that naturally, of course, but Alex thinks his dad's a bit obsessive about it lately. It's early May – in a good year rain would be on its way by now.

'Yeah, just me.'

He walks up the steps and Tangi flops beside the bench. 'What have you been up to today?' Alex asks. He doesn't ask how his dad is, as it seems like he often can't explain.

'Gave the ute a service. Changed the oil.' His dad smiles, and Alex relaxes. Today's a good day then. His dad seems happier when he can work on machinery and engines. Dad's mate Roger was probably over, too.

'That's great.'

'What about you?'

'Ag science was interesting. This Year Twelve guy came in to tell us about his research project — saltbush, how it's high fibre, and can uptake salt, reducing soil salinity. It's drought-resistant, but it can survive in soils with salinity that would kill most other plants.' Alex can't stop. 'It gives other plants a better chance to grow.'

'S'pose he reckons we should grow saltbush like a crop, eh? This the Schmidt boy?'

'Josh, yeah. He's got good ideas. Maybe we could do more like that – help with the drought . . .'

Alex trails off, seeing his dad's eyes darken. It's as if he's shut off a light inside.

'Sorry, Dad. I've been raving on and making you tired.'

His dad waves him away. 'Go and exercise Jago. Maybe I'll help feed the chooks when you get back.'

'Sure, Dad, you take it easy.'

Alex drops his bag in his room and heads to the kitchen. He pours a glass of cold water and gulps it down. It's autumn, but still twenty-five degrees outside. Should be cooler by now.

His mum isn't home; she's been doing shifts three times a week at the local pub, cooking. Their town is half an hour's drive away, and meal prep starts at four. That's what puts food on the table here. She usually leaves a note. None today.

Tangi skips around Alex, ready for a run after hearing the mention of Jago. Alex heads for the shed that counts as the stable. He hears the whinny before he reaches it.

He often wonders if Jago is lonely after his big sister, Lily, took their mare, Posie, with her to live with their grandparents in Adelaide. She and Grandad go for rides and keep the horses in a stable north of the suburbs. If she were here they'd be doing this together.

How could Lily bear to leave? He'd miss the sky at night, the sunrises, the sunsets, the cobalt blue that's always there during the day, even if he hasn't felt as though there's much colour in his life lately.

'Hi, Jago.' Alex scratches Jago's brown head and the white splotch on his forehead. Jago plants a whiskery kiss on his face. 'Pleased to see me, eh?'

Alex doesn't bother with a saddle today, just takes the bridle off the hook and puts the bit in the horse's mouth. 'Where shall we go, you two?'

Jago turns his brown eyes on him and nickers. Jago likes Rocky Peak. So does Alex. It's the only landmark of interest in a flat landscape.

He jumps on Jago's back and turns him south. They canter, then full-on gallop.

Tangi loves a run just as much as Jago, but she can't keep up. Her paws get sore after a while. Always sits down halfway there under the shadiest eucalyptus tree and waits until Alex returns, then trots back with them.

Riding Jago always gives Alex a reprieve from his thoughts. Thoughts about whether Lily is happy away from the property, because he certainly wouldn't be. And about his dad, who's been unwell for over a year now. When will he get better? Jago is racing across the paddock, and the wind in Alex's face blows everything out of his mind. He even laughs as Jago's hooves pound across the cracked ground.

Rocky Peak looms in front of them, and they weave their way to the top. There they rest, Jago checking out the ground for blades of grass, and Alex staring down at the view of their property. He loves it up here. From this point he can see the Flinders Ranges to the north, purple in the distance. This hill straddles the boundary between their property and that of the Gibsons next door.

The Gibsons' place is up for lease. Another farmer bitten the dust and gone south to find work. The drought got too much – their bore dried up. Hard to know if the water will come again or not. The Gibsons had four young kids – their leaving made a huge dent at school, and it meant they lost a teacher as well. It was bad for the town too – fewer people buying stuff is not good for businesses, and the Gibsons are not the only ones who have left.

Looks like fences going up at the Gibsons where Alex hasn't seen any before. Maybe someone's moved in.

His great-great-grandfather called their property Spring Park because there was a spring near where the bore is. That's a joke now. The spring dried up eighty years ago. Alex wonders if the land looked like a park back then. When he was younger he could see green paddocks from up here by the beginning of May, but right now it's still warm and dry like the end of summer, not mid-autumn. The drought has brought more whirly-whirlies and soil erosion.

He sighs at the dusty brown landscape before him. They've had drought for quite a few years. It was extra bad in 2019, which was when they had attention from the government and media. Even though people down south seem to think the drought's broken, Alex's family still can't put a hay crop in.

When he's older he wants to help make the farm more sustainable, but what can be done without rain? Moist soil is needed for the land to be sustainable. Even the creek has nothing in it except fallen trees. He glances to the north-east, where the tree line of the creek breaks up the northern paddocks.

At least it's cooler up here and he can see the paddocks around the house near the huge ghost gum his great-great-grandfather planted when he built it. The ghost gum is magnificent, especially when it's shining in the moonlight.

His gaze shifts to the empty dam to the east. He's seen no water in that since he was young, either. Alex doesn't like going near the mound to the right of it. Nor does Dad. Too many bad memories.

He pats Jago's neck. 'What'd'ya reckon, boy? What can help the property get better, and Dad too?' Jago snorts. 'Yeah, I can't think of much either.'

Just then Jago's ears twitch and his shoulders shiver. 'What is it, boy?' Then Alex hears it too.

A stone rolls down behind him, and another, then there's a fall of shale. Jago's showing the whites of his eyes. 'Hey, boy, it's okay.' Alex pats Jago on the neck, uses soothing words, but it doesn't work. Jago turns in a circle, his ears back, tail swishing, his front legs ready to rear. 'Steady, boy, steady.'

Alex has to keep calm so Jago can settle, but he doesn't know what's coming. His heart is galloping.

They face the direction of the sounds, hear a growl. An animal must be moving up the other side, and Jago doesn't like it. It's not thumping like a kangaroo. Too heavy for a dingo, which are rarely seen due to the Dingo Fence.

'Who's there?' Alex calls, in case it's a person.

Jago turns another circle, then backs up too close to the edge. Alex glances over his shoulder. Stones scatter and sheer away below them. 'Easy, boy, easy.'

No one answers. Not a person, then.

Jago is snorting, tossing his head. If he backs up any further they'll go over the side. Alex keeps the reins short, but Jago is lifting his head higher, his nostrils flaring.

There's a growl, close by. Then the animal shows itself, teeth bared, and creeps forward on to the edge. It snarls at Jago.

It has to be a feral dog. It's huge, in poor condition, but surely it wouldn't attack a horse.

Jago rears. Alex isn't expecting it and has to scrabble to stay on. He should have used a saddle. He slips.

'Ooph!'

The wind is knocked out of him. He's dragged a few metres before he lets go of the reins, but he's on the same level as the dog now.

Its gaze locks on him and it growls, low and guttural. It edges forward until it's fully on the track, closer to Alex. Its front legs quiver, readying for attack. Alex averts his eyes – staring at an aggressive dog will only make it worse. There's nothing else he can do, no sticks he can grab to protect himself.

Jago squeals, lowers his head and charges the dog.

'No!' Alex shouts. It'll attack Jago for sure. He can imagine those fangs sinking into Jago's neck.

Jago rears over the dog. His hooves crash down on its front paws, and it yelps. Jago rears again and the dog springs away, back down the rise. Jago shakes his head up and down, then nuzzles Alex's hair.

'Ow.' Alex's lower back hurts as he manages to stand up. Has he broken anything? His legs seem to work. No sharp pains, but his muscles will be sore for yonks.

'Phew, are you Wonder Horse or what?' Alex has only seen Jago act that way once before, with a snake last October – a time of year when snakes are hungry and aggressive. Jago is used to dogs, yet somehow he knew this one was not a friend. 'Thank you, Jago. You just saved my bacon.'

That dog sure was a nasty piece of work – so hungry it would hold up a horse or a person. Seeing a feral dog so near their place is worrying, but he's surprised at how shaken up he is. It's well known that the drought is bringing wild animals closer to properties as there's little for them to eat, but this is getting too close.

'Come on, Jago, let's go home.' Alex leads Jago to a rocky outcrop and climbs on a rock to reach the horse's back. 'Ouch.' He's never had to do that before; usually he can spring up, even without a saddle to grip on to.

On the way back, Tangi joins them as they pass the tall eucalypt. Jago's still tossing his head. Alex knows he should tell his dad about the feral dog, but it might trigger a bad reaction. It doesn't take much for Dad to fall apart at the moment. Will it always be like this?

Two

||||||||||||||||||||||||||||||||||||||||||||||||||||||||||||||||||||||||||||||||||||||

Dad's not on the veranda when Alex gets back from rubbing Jago down. *Guess he's forgotten about helping with the feed-run.*

Alex always feeds the animals before dinner. He has a system: Jago first, then pellets for the chooks – they love scraps, too – collect the eggs, scrub them, put them in the cool room on egg trays. His mum takes them to the General Store in town when she has a shift at the pub. After that Alex waters his herb and veggie garden when the sun's low to minimise evaporation, and finally, he feeds Tangi on the veranda by her kennel.

Today, on impulse, he decides to check the sheep have enough hay before he feeds the chooks – save his mum doing it tomorrow. At the same time he can see if there's water in the troughs. There's not enough feed for the sheep in the paddocks because of the drought, so they're hand-fed.

Alex goes to the machinery shed where the ute and quad bike are kept, and finds the quad-bike key under the front mat. He rides it to the hay shed, grabs a hay bale by the twine and hoists it onto the trailer. When the bales run out, they buy in more from down south where farmers can still do cropping. Mum's doing her best by working at the pub, but she doesn't make enough for hay. They have to rely on the wool sales to cover that.

His back muscles complain again. 'Ouch.'

Alex drives through the paddock that has the dam in it. His parents don't discuss this paddock. Things are different now with Dad feeling depressed a lot of the time and not able to work like he used to. Alex has been able and willing to help with his dad's chores – at least they're together.

How could Mum even suggest he leave and study in the city, like Lily, or in some big rural town like Port Augusta? That's over a hundred kilometres away – he'd only get home for weekends. He doesn't think he would survive, and probably Mum and Dad wouldn't either. Dad misses Lily too much as it is.

Besides, the area school says he can study online. Many senior high school students in rural districts are doing that now because of the pandemic. COVID-19 has affected farmers and townspeople too with fewer jobs, fewer shops and cafes open, which in turn keeps tourists away. No one's travelling much at the moment.

Drought is second nature to Alex – he hardly knows anything different – but there was the bushfire on top of that, then the pandemic. It's been a triple whammy. His dad couldn't— But Alex shoves that thought out of his mind. It never helps to think *what if things were different*. It's the way it is, and they just have to get on with it.

The sheep come running when they hear the quad bike. Lanky is the first to reach him, baa-ing.

He scratches her on the head. 'Hey to you too, Lanky. Have you been getting on with all your friends or are you still ignoring them?' She follows him to the quad bike and baas again and he drives off. 'You miss riding with me, eh? You're too big now, Lanky, sorry.'

His dad taught him how to drive the quad bike and the ute. *Only on the property*, he said. But Mum has the ute today, since they had to sell her car. Too expensive to keep up the registration.

After Alex ensures the sheep have enough hay, he checks the level of water in the tank with his hand on its shadow side. The bottom third is cooler to his touch – still water left. The trough has a float – while there's water in the tank, there'll be water in the trough. It's a five-thousand-litre tank, so they'll have to cart water from the bore tank soon. In this weather the sheep drink five thousand litres in a week. In summer it only lasts a few days.

Because of the drought they can only run one sheep to six hectares on natural feed. That means only thirty or so ewes in a paddock like this at one hundred and eighty hectares, so now they are hand-fed and more sheep can live in a paddock. When he was younger there was enough natural feed to sustain over a hundred sheep in a paddock like this one. Sheep farms in this district need to be big enough to provide enough feed; theirs is three thousand hectares. Mum says a property needs two thousand sheep to make a living, but Alex doesn't think they've ever had that many. Since the bushfire they only have four hundred ewes left. It's been a challenge to make enough money from sheep and wool sales to keep the farm going. And now that the sheep are hand-fed, the cost of hay makes it even less profitable.

A few kookaburras laugh in the gum trees, and Alex smiles – they don't often come up this far. His grandpa told him that if kookaburras laugh late in the afternoon like this, it will rain the next day. 'Ha, someone needs to tell the rain to listen, hey, Tangi?' She grins at him like it's a good joke. Alex wishes it was just a joke.

He finds the eggs have already been collected. Dad sure is having a good day.

Alex puts Tangi's food in a bowl and takes it out to the veranda. She waits politely until he says to eat it, but he never delays giving her the go-ahead. That's another thing his dad taught him: *Look after the animals first, then eat.* Alex pats her. 'When you're a bit older and we get a new pup, you'll be allowed inside all the time, Tangi. You'll be retired!' She looks up at him for a second, then scoffs the rest of her dinner.

It's dusk and a white owl glides into the sky from the ghost gum. Alex catches his breath. The owl never fails to move him.

Inside, Alex takes out three dinners his mum has made from the freezer, puts one in the microwave, and sets the table. His mum says to keep things as normal as possible for his dad's sake even while she's at the pub.

'Dad,' Alex calls. He hears a murmur, and finds his dad in the lounge room watching the news. 'It's time for tea. Are you hungry?'

His dad shrugs. 'Darn news, always something bad happening.' Alex's heart sinks. The news often changes his dad's mood.

'C'mon, we'll eat together.' Alex hopes Dad doesn't refuse. He's not sure what to do when that happens. But his dad flicks the remote and stands up, steadying himself on the back of the couch, and shuffles into the kitchen. Alex puts the second of the meals in the microwave. 'Thanks for collecting the eggs, Dad.'

His dad nods. 'Thanks for feeding the sheep.'

So he does take notice. At times Alex feels he's sunk in a world of his own.

They eat together silently until his dad says, 'Heard from Lily?'

'Last I knew, she was on a PE camp.'

'She has a lot of those.'

Alex smiles at him. Dad seems to have forgotten the bad news on TV. That must be a good sign. Maybe he's getting better. But Alex knows not to get excited. At times his dad seems well, but the next day he can be a different person.

It all began with the drought, which in turn caused the bushfire early last year. Dad had to shoot the burnt sheep, hundreds of them, burying them next to the dam. He has never been himself since. Before that he stood tall, efficient in his farming, teaching Alex skills he'll need. On good days he can still do some of that, but it's like walking a tightrope not knowing from one day to the next what his mood will be.

Later, Alex is in his room when he hears the screen door bang. Mum's home. He always feels relief when she's in the house. He gives her a minute or two to get a coffee and put her dinner in the microwave. Then he shuts his laptop and goes into the kitchen.

'Hey, Mum.' Her eyes crinkle, but Alex can tell she's tired. Her brown hair is scraped into a knot, and there are dark patches under her eyes. He gives her a hug – he's a head taller than her now. 'Work okay?'

She nods, takes a sip of coffee. Then she sighs. 'Good to be home.'

'Anyone book in?' It's only Thursday night; people usually come on weekends. Their district is called the Gateway to the Outback, so people expect bush tucker.

'A family on their way to the Flinders, camping. A few others wanting emu steaks. One lot said they wanted an "explorer's platter".' She smiles. 'Emu, kangaroo and camel. Maybe we should add that to the menu.' Often his mum visits the dining room to meet people, or to clean up. 'Few guys in the bar had dinner – looked like a meeting. Talking about the drought, what to do . . .' Her voice trails away.

Talk of the drought is never easy in their house. Alex is almost used to it as a way of life, but his mum remembers better days and wants them back.

She asks about Dad. 'How's Tom?'

'He's asleep in front of the TV. We had a good evening. He ate his tea.'

She smiles and clasps his hand. 'Thank you, Alex. I worry leaving you alone when he's like this.'

'He'll get better, won't he, Mum?'

She grimaces. 'He's suffered a dreadful trauma. It'll just take time.'

Alex can tell she's just repeating things the doctor has said, but he truly wants to believe it. He wants his dad back the way he was.

Alex wants to tell his mum about the feral dog, but decides she's too tired and kisses her on the cheek instead. 'Night, Mum. I'll see you in the morning.' He says it like he's got studying to do and she nods, even though his school doesn't give homework before senior high.

'Night, Alexander.'

Back in his room, he opens the laptop, then changes his mind. It's not too late to send a text to Lily. Then he can tell Dad some good news. Not for the first time, Alex thinks his sister should be here. It would help Dad, he's sure of it.

Hey, sis, Dad was asking today how you are.

He reads a whole chapter of *The Hobbit* before she replies.

Is he getting better?

He had a good day today. But he gets tired.

Lily is the only one he can talk to about Dad. What would he say at school if he was asked about his dad? Nothing. But even Lily doesn't say much about Dad either.

Nan and Grandad okay?

All good. Grandad forgets where he's put stuff.

Alex thinks their dad is just as bad at the moment.

See ya, Lil. Wish you were here.

Lily just sends a sleepy emoticon in reply.

He hopes she doesn't think he's complaining, but the truth is, he's still annoyed that she left to study in the city.

Oh well, time to turn in. During the week Alex goes to bed early as he needs to wake before sunrise to do the morning feed run and help his mum – his dad isn't bright in the mornings. The bus comes at seven-thirty to do the long trip around all the properties picking up the farm kids in time for school. The town kids have it easy – they get to sleep in. But Alex would never trade more sleep for his life on Spring Park.

Three

Alex springs awake. A hand is shaking him hard.
'Get off me!' he shouts, his eyes still shut with sleep.

'Alex, get up!'

His heart is thumping. He opens his eyes to see his
dad, trembling, his eyes wide with fear.

'Dad?' Alex sits up. 'What wrong?'

'I can smell smoke. We have to save the sheep.'

'Dad, it's okay, the fire's gone now.' He gets up and
puts an arm around his dad's back. 'Let's get you back to
bed, it's too early.' Alex tries not to show the fright he's had.

'You sure the fire's out?'

'Absolutely. No need to worry.'

His dad walks with him back to the main bedroom,
his feet scuffling on the pine floor like a grandfather's,
not a forty-five-year-old's. His mum is putting her
slippers on. 'Oh, thank goodness. There you are, Tom –
come back to bed.'

She turns to Alex. 'I'm sorry, Alexander, I didn't
realise he was gone.'

'It's okay, Mum.'

But it isn't. It used to be him who'd run into his parents' bedroom after a bad dream. This is the wrong way round.

Alex finds it hard to get back to sleep, and it seems like only minutes pass before it's time to get up and do his feed run. As he comes back in from the paddock, he sees his mum trying to get his dad to the breakfast table. 'I don't want to eat,' Dad says.

'We're having scrambled eggs today, Dad,' Alex says. 'Bacon too. You like that. Baked beans.' The promise of beans does it. Dad sits at the table, but doesn't look up while Alex helps his mum in the kitchen.

There's the sound of a ute pulling up, a knock at the door. Roger, their neighbour and Dad's friend, pokes his head inside.

'Come in,' Alex calls.

'G'day, mate.' Roger sits beside Dad while Alex serves them both eggs, bacon, baked beans and toast.

Roger tries to visit once a week to do things with Dad on the property, or take him to medical appointments if Mum's working. Getting to appointments is hard to manage with Dad. At least his counsellor rings him on the phone. His dad seems to cope with that better than on Zoom. No eye contact. And besides, Zoom often drops out when the internet connection's bad.

'Thanks for coming,' Alex says. Today is a good day for Roger to come – his dad isn't coping and Mum doesn't allow Alex to miss school to help at home.

Roger looks up and nods. He seems to understand Alex's meaning. 'What say we go over to the Men's Shed today, Tom? Some of the blokes are planning on restoring a car. You'd be up for that?'

Alex's dad shakes his head, but Roger isn't deterred. 'Then we'll work here. The volunteers helped a lot with our fences after the fire, but there's more work to be done.'

Alex holds his breath. Roger's game mentioning fencing. He knows that his dad can't handle working with the sheep yet.

Since his dad still doesn't answer, Alex says, 'The water level is down in the tanks. It could wait a few days, but it would be helpful if you and Dad carted the water from the bore tank to the paddocks. I'm not allowed to drive the truck yet and it's a big job for Mum.'

Mum raises her eyebrows at him, and Alex isn't sure if she's happy with him for suggesting that, but it's true.

Roger doesn't miss a beat. 'No worries. We can get onto that, can't we, Tom?' When he doesn't get a response, he glances up. 'You have a hard night, Rachael?'

She nods slightly.

'Righto,' Roger says. 'Let's get cracking then. C'mon, Tom, let's get the job done. We'll both feel bonza after.'

He ushers Dad out the screen door onto the veranda. 'Here's your boots, mate.'

Alex picks up his backpack, kisses his mum. As he and Tangi walk to the main road, he thinks about how yesterday his dad could've put his boots on himself; he didn't need to be jollied into it like a kid.

When he sees the dust of the bus, Alex gives Tangi a pat. 'Go home, girl.' Tangi yips and starts walking towards the house, stopping to look back as the bus pulls off the road. 'Go home,' Alex reminds her, and watches her trot off as he climbs the steps into the bus. At the top he's met by Harry's sparkling dark eyes. 'She's a good dog, mate.'

'How come you're on the bus before me?'

'Dad dropped me at Freddy's place on his way down to the city. His mum helped me sort out the algebra.'

Alex glances across the aisle at Freddy, who's grinning at them. 'Mum used to be a teacher,' Freddy says. 'I get my smarts from her.'

'Year Five stuff is easy,' Alex says. 'Wait till you're in Year Seven.'

He sits down and winces. His muscles still hurt.

'What happened to you, mate?' Harry sure is sharp.

Alex blows out a breath. 'Had a run-in with a feral dog.'

'Naah.' Harry's eyes grow even wider.

'Too right I did. On Rocky Peak. It almost went for Jago. He got spooked and I fell off.' As Harry frowns at him, disbelieving, Alex adds, 'The dog saw me on the ground—'

'Strewth, easier prey, mate.'

'Yeah, but Jago went for it just in time, stamped on its leg.'

Alex skips a breath, thinking how things could have turned out worse with his mum away. Only his dad knew he was out riding – would he have noticed if Alex hadn't come home for dinner?

'Blow me down, never heard of that before.'

Alex grins at Harry's colourful phrase, learned from his stockman dad.

'The drought's done that, brung the ferals closer,' Harry says. 'Like the camels up north trying to find water, causin' trouble on stations.' The cattle station Harry's dad works on isn't as big as stations up north that are measured by square kilometres, but it still seems huge to Alex at nineteen thousand hectares.

Alex pulls out his art journal and Harry bends closer. 'Whatcha drawin'?'

Alex shrugs. 'Just doodling.' He draws a comic image of Harry with wings like a galah.

'Ha. You're the galah, mate.' Harry takes the pencil and draws a caricature of Alex with willie wagtail feathers. 'Willie wagtails are special mates. They can bring messages, sometimes good, usually bad.'

'What sort of message would I bring, then?'

'Dunno. I'm just drawin', like you.'

Drawing helps pass the rest of the hour's trip to school while the younger kids play games on tablets and chat or read.

Foundation to Year Three are lining up outside their classroom by the time the bus pulls in. Alex and Harry are the only Year Sevens and don't have to line up, so they walk down the path to their building. Their school is small, but they have more than enough buildings for classes and even have an art studio. As they pass the dozen little kids, Harry gives an imitation of a crow: 'Aa, aa, aaaaa.' All the kids giggle, even the Year Fours to Sixes.

The high school kids' class will not be impressed, so the boys quietly walk onto their veranda. Summer in Year Ten and Tara in Year Nine are putting their bags away in their lockers as Alex and Harry turn up. Alex is still grinning from Harry acting like a crow. 'You're such a galah,' he whispers to Harry. Harry nickers like Jago, which makes Alex grin wider.

Summer turns and sees them. She flicks her blond fringe out of her eyes, glaring. 'Why are you two acting like clowns?'

Tara screws up her nose as she looks at Alex. 'Why don't they leave the Year Sevens with the Year Sixes?' She pulls her wavy brown hair into a ponytail and follows Summer inside.

Harry takes a bow. 'Welcome to our happy class,' he says to Alex as if he were new.

Alex can't stop grinning. It's always good being around Harry. He makes problems seem like puffs of smoke that disappear in the breeze. Even Summer and Tara can't annoy Alex today.

Those girls have tried every trick to pick on them. Tripping them up, telling the teacher if they do anything wrong, not helping them understand their work when they know how to do it. When Summer's cross with them the atmosphere in the class changes. Alex can't understand why she's so mean to them. She looks like she has everything going for her – she lives in town, she has her friends. But she hasn't included Alex and Harry in her circle. Alex doesn't like sides in a small school like theirs. Everyone needs to get along.

After school is footy practice. The boys put their gear on and race out to the oval. Harry can barely wait for footy. 'It's amazing how my old man goes on about me helping on the station, but he doesn't mind me playing footy.'

'Maybe he thinks even if you're a galah in maths you can always get a career playing footy.'

Harry laughs. 'Maybe he hopes I'll follow in Eddy Betts's footsteps, hey? He was my old man's favourite player.'

'I can come to practice, but I'll only be a reserve this season.' This would be a good time to tell Harry about his dad's illness and the extra work it means, but Alex doesn't know how to start.

Charlie, Harry's dad, turns up in the station's Land Cruiser and watches the last of the practice. He's still in his stockman duds, and with his black ponytail and half-grey goatee he looks like a cool dude. 'Get your bags, boys,' he says at the end. 'Nice ball skills,' he adds, nodding to Alex. Alex knows he'll never be as good as Harry, but the praise makes him feel warm anyway. Charlie's an expert on footy, and full of life like Harry.

Alex hopes his dad will be equally kind to Harry. It's nerve-wracking wondering how his dad will be when they turn up. Especially when Alex hasn't told Harry about his illness.

When they arrive at Alex's place, Charlie and Harry come inside. Charlie's almost as tall as Dad, and he puts an arm around him. 'G'day, mate. How're ya goin?'

Dad blinks, then says, 'Want to watch the game?'

'Is the sky blue? Just for a while, though. Harry and I have to rise with the crows tomorrow.'

'Cattle work?'

Charlie nods.

'Coffee, Charlie?' Alex says.

'Too right. Can you make it as well as your mum?'

'Almost. Dad, one for you too?'

'Nah, might keep me awake.' Alex stares at him; was that a joke? Or does he wake up often during the night? No wonder he's tired in the daytime.

Harry goes with Alex to the kitchen and gets out the Milo. 'I've got the kettle on.'

'Thanks.' Alex tries to get the milk to steam up properly. He can't draw fancy shapes in the froth like his mum does. He takes the coffee to Charlie and the boys take their Milos to Alex's room.

'How about we play Minecraft on your laptop?' Harry suggests.

'Okay.' Alex enjoys not thinking about anything except the fun of creating new worlds. An hour goes by before Charlie gives a hoy through the doorway. 'Harry, time to go. Port's winning, so it's a good time to leave.' He chuckles. 'If Eddie Betts was still with the Crows this would be a different game.'

After they've driven off, Alex sits with his dad to watch the rest of the match. His dad's a Port Adelaide man and he urges them on, but the game turns. It's tense, and Alex glances at his dad. Watching this game probably isn't the best idea. 'Stop holding the ball!' his dad yells. 'Kick it, you mug! What's that umpire doing?'

Alex sighs with relief when the siren goes, even if Mum says any emotion is better expressed than none at all. The Crows win by a point. Dad is not happy.

'C'mon, Dad, let's go to bed.'

His dad mumbles, 'They gotta lift their game.' He starts blaming players, then the coach. He never used to let footy get him down. He'd always say it was just a game.

'This way, Dad – toilet, teeth.' It's what Dad used to say to him when it was time for bed when he was little. Alex scrubs out that thought.

He holds his dad steady as he stands. He's a bit wobbly, but his feet get moving with Alex pulling a little. Not too much – his dad doesn't like being pushed. Fair enough, too. He gets his dad in bed just as his mum walks in.

'I could have done that, Alexander.'

'Thought I'd save you a job.'

His mum stares at him, and Alex winces. Is that what Dad is now? Just a job?

Four

|||||||||||||||||||||||||||||||||||||||||||||||||||||||||||||||||||||||||||||||

Next morning, Mr Clarke, their maths, science and home group teacher, is setting up tasks on their screens. Alex and Harry are learning algebra, and it's proving tricky for both of them. 'Numbers are enough trouble without little letters as well,' Harry complains, and Alex agrees.

When they're all in, Mr Clarke checks the roll on his computer. With only ten of them he doesn't have to read out names.

'Now,' Mr Clarke says, 'a new student will be starting today. She's at the office enrolling.'

Harry and Alex glance at each other. Alex wonders which year level this new student will be in. The girls are quiet; Alex catches Summer raising her eyebrows at Tara, whose face has darkened. He wonders what they know about the new girl. In town, news travels as fast as a flock of cockatoos.

'Alex, Harry, our new student will be in Year Seven, so you two can go to the office now to bring her to class.'

Alex and Harry look at each other, like, *Us? He chooses us?* They hardly ever get chosen for important stuff like this. Tara mouths 'losers' at them as they push their chairs out.

'What do you think she'll be like?' Harry says on the way over. He sounds hopeful, and Alex grins.

'All the girls in South Australia can't be like Summer and Tara, eh?'

'Guess not, but we're going to have a lot more to do with her than them, since she's in our year level.' Harry grabs Alex's arm. 'What if she joins Summer's circle and we have three girls picking on us? You know, like them not telling us the class was having that picnic last term and we missed out.'

'Yeah. And when they stayed on the computers in the library all lunchtime and we couldn't get our projects done in time.'

They both shrug.

When they turn up at the office, the girl is sitting in the reception area on the only chair. She has a long brown ponytail and olive skin, and she's already wearing the school uniform: blue shorts, blue-and-white shirt.

Alex realises he's staring. 'Hey, I'm Alex.' He bumps Harry.

'Harry.'

'Are you the welcoming committee?' As she stands, the girl smiles and both boys relax. She comes up to Alex's shoulder, the same height as Harry.

'I'm Bonnie Saleh.' She looks like a person who can stand on her own two feet, as Alex's dad used to say.

'G'day.' Harry shifts his feet, then grins. All the girls in their class are older, and ignore them when they're not picking on them (that's Summer and Tara), but here's a girl their own age for the first time since last year.

Alex shows her where to put her bag on the veranda, and where the loos are. She looks a bit disorientated, but nods vaguely. Harry hits the nail on the head. 'Ever been to school before, Bonnie?'

She stares at him, and Alex sees a sheen in her eyes – the faintest touch of terror? 'It'll be okay,' he says. 'You did School of the Air?'

She nods. 'I could do the work at my own pace.' Alex knows what she's thinking. He would too: *What if I can't keep up?*

'You won't have any trouble here,' Harry says. 'Alex and me are galahs.'

'Hey.' Alex play-punches him. He sees Bonnie smile and the day is right side up again.

'That's what Mr Clarke says to us at least once a week.' Harry's eyes dance.

Bonnie giggles. 'That often?' Alex hopes she can tell Harry is pulling her leg.

Harry has sure saved the day.

'The Year Eights to Tens are in our class too,' Alex explains. 'They have their own screens for maths and English. We do subjects like science, HASS, technologies and health and PE together. Just our assignments are different. There's a Year Eleven student, and a Year Twelve, too, but they do their own subjects online from different schools.'

Harry says, 'Alex's sister, Lily, was in this class last year.'

Bonnie turns to Alex. 'She graduated?'

'Nah, went to the city to study.'

Bonnie looks surprised, like, *Who'd want to do that?* But Alex doesn't feel like sticking up for Lily today.

As they lead her into class, Alex watches Summer and Tara taking note of Bonnie. She's noticed them staring and purses her lips.

Mr Clarke gives Bonnie the run-down on work and gives her some sheets to fill in to see how much she knows. Bonnie seems happier and sits at Harry and Alex's round table to work on the questions.

At recess, Summer and Tara stride up to her. Alex wills them to be kind.

Summer flicks her hair to the side. 'I'm Summer. You must be Bonnie Saleh?' She doesn't wait for Bonnie to answer. It's not like there's any other new girl at school. 'Mr Clarke said I should look after you at lunch.' She glances at Alex and Harry like she's saved Bonnie from a fate worse than death.

'Thanks,' Bonnie says.

'This is Tara.'

Tara just stares at her. Bonnie nods.

'Hey, Sophie,' Alex says as another girl comes over. Sophie lifts her chin at him and her dark curls bounce. Then she grins at Bonnie. 'I'm in Year Nine. I'm so glad you've come. We need more girls in this class.'

'There are already more girls,' Alex says.

'So?' Tara says, still without smiling at Bonnie. Alex

wonders what's wrong with her. Is it because Bonnie's in Year Seven with them? Surely not. Tara's acting like she knows something about Bonnie and doesn't like whatever it is.

Alex, Bonnie and Harry get talking on the bus that afternoon. Turns out Bonnie's family has taken over the lease on Gibsons' place next door to Alex. 'Why didn't you come on the bus this morning?' Alex asks.

'Dad brought me – he thought it would be less stressful.'

'Harry laughs. 'You hadn't met us yet, hey.'

'Why don't you both get off the bus at my place?' she asks. 'My father would drive you home. You could see the camels.'

Harry raises his eyebrows at Alex. 'Camels?' He shakes his head. 'Can't, I'm sorry. I need to help my old man with the cattle after school.'

'His dad works on the station down the road from my place,' Alex answers the question on Bonnie's face. 'I reckon I could come over. I don't think my parents would mind as long as I do my jobs when I get home. My dog will be waiting at the bus stop, so I'll go home first.'

'Great.' Bonnie gives Alex a double high-five as she gets off the bus.

After greeting Tangi at the gate, and checking on his dad, Alex saddles up Jago and rides him over Rocky Peak to Bonnie's place. He thinks of his dad, half-asleep on the couch – he'll be okay until he gets back.

After Rocky Peak they trot to the next paddock, opening and closing gates on the way. Alex can do it from horseback for the easier gates. Some are so complicated, involving lengths of pipe and wire, that he has to dismount for them. They pick their way down the other side to the boundary. There's a gate at the bottom – a new fence. High enough to keep wild camels in.

Bonnie's house is closer to the road than his. Looks like a transportable, with large open windows and the usual tin roof and a veranda built on the west. The Gibson place is only about six hundred hectares. Maybe that's enough for camels. Halfway across the paddock Alex can see the fences he spotted from Rocky Peak the other day – they're higher than usual fences. He guesses that's for yarding the camels.

The closer they ride, the more skittish Jago becomes. Alex has to hold the reins firmly to get Jago to go forward at a trot. Jago shakes his head up and down, stepping sideways. He tries every trick he knows without actually throwing Alex off. He's acting so scared that Alex looks around for a feral dog, not that he expects to see one again. They finally arrive at the house, where Bonnie meets them. She's wearing blue jeans and a T-shirt, and has a light brown hat similar to his Akubra.

'Beautiful horse,' she says.

Jago snorts and doesn't even say hello to Bonnie. 'He's not behaving like himself today,' Alex says as he dismounts.

She leads them over to the camel yards. 'Come and meet my camel, Ruby.'

Ruby is a reddish colour. She kisses the top of Bonnie's head, then ambles towards Alex. It's too much for Jago. He rears suddenly, rips the reins from Alex's grip and gallops away to the paddock, clearing the house fence. Alex gives chase and calls to him, but Jago doesn't stop until he's at the gate to the next paddock. He waits there, gives a whinny as if to say, *I'll just stay here if you don't mind*, and calmly searches for dry grass to nibble.

Alex walks back to Bonnie. 'He's okay now, but he's never run off like that before. He seemed terrified.' At least with the feral dog Jago stood his ground to protect Alex.

'I'm sorry,' Bonnie says. 'I should have warned you that horses usually don't get along with camels at first.'

Alex's eyes squint, watching Jago, but he doesn't want to spoil the visit. He turns to Bonnie. 'The yards your dad is building are impressive.'

'Yep – he had to start before we came, so we could contain the camels when we brought them.' Maybe people know about the camels, then. Kids in town would have seen the trucks. Bonnie continues, 'This is for the young ones, or females ready to give birth after winter. Most are happy grazing in the paddocks.'

Alex looks at her incredulously. 'Grazing? You're trying to put a crop in? No one crops up here except for hay.'

Bonnie shakes her head. 'Nup, they don't need crops. We have to feed them, usually, hay and stuff, but they do like saltbush.'

'Plenty of that.'

She looks around. 'This isn't big like the station we were living on near Farina up north – at least it's easier to find the adult camels when we need to.'

'I'd like to see those places up north,' Alex says.

She glances at him. 'Maybe you can come when we go to the winter camel races at Marree.'

'Does your dad train them to race?'

'Not all. Some are sold as pets, some are used for treks. Dad runs a few of those in spring. People from down south want to see the wildflowers miraculously appear in the desert.'

'A trek sounds like fun.'

She nods. 'I've been a few times when he's taken families. Once a year he runs a trek for a science expedition.'

'Hoy, Bonnie.' A man in a khaki shirt and shorts, younger than his dad, waves from the fence he's constructing. His hands are full with a length of railing and a drill. An older man stands nearby, his hair pure white, topped with a faded cap. Alex follows Bonnie over.

'Would you like a hand, Mr Saleh?' Alex asks after Bonnie has introduced her dad and pop.

'Sure, you hold the end of that rail while I drill a hole here. Pop isn't feeling helpful today.'

Alex glances at the old man and thinks Bonnie's dad must be joking – what could that ancient guy do? Pop moves away towards a calf that looks a bit lost. Guess they haven't been here long.

Mr Saleh looks up. 'And call me Sully, mate. Everyone's called our family that for generations. They couldn't pronounce Saleh.'

'Where do you get the camels?'

Sully finishes the drilling before he replies, probably because his mouth is full of bolts. 'I catch 'em in the desert.'

'They're feral?' Alex gazes at the camels crowding around checking what Sully is doing. 'They don't look it.' One reaches over and kisses Alex on the cheek. It makes him start, and Bonnie laughs. 'That's Gertrude, she's very affectionate.'

'They were feral once,' Sully says, 'even Gertrude. Not the young ones like Ruby – we've bred those.'

Bonnie says, 'We do a muster each year for half-grown ones, then Dad retrains them.'

Alex gazes at Sully in amazement.

Bonnie chuckles. 'He's a camel whisperer.'

'That's – well, I've not heard anything like it before.' Alex remembers what his dad said. 'They cause so much damage up north because of the drought. And end up as dog meat, you know . . .' *The only good camel is a dead one*, some station owners say. He can't say that, not with Ruby snuffling his head like Jago does.

'Yep,' Sully says. 'Bonnie's mum and I – we couldn't stand it. We thought we'd save the ones we could. You can do a lot with camels. It's not just pub food, treks and Christmas nativity parties. We're trialling camel dairy products.' He points at some yards further away. 'Welcome to the first camel dairy in the mid north.'

'Don't you need lots of water for dairies?'

'We'll try to sink a new bore. This place will be more viable if there's water, so fingers crossed we find some.'

Alex nods.

'Camels protect cattle and sheep from wild dogs,' Bonnie says.

'Like alpacas?' Alex says.

'Yep. Plus they eat anything.'

Sully laughs. 'They're good for weed management.'

There are still weeds on Alex's place, even though it hasn't rained properly in ages.

Weeds are adaptable. 'You see, Alex, we care about the environment and right now camels are a part of the environment, so we're trying different ways that they can fit in. For us it's not an option to just get rid of animals – we need to discover how they can be useful.'

Alex nods slowly. 'So why do horses hate camels?'

Sully grins. 'Just the way it is, always has been. Camels are huge, intimidating, even if most of them are sooks. Then there's the smell, which seems to affect horses. But I know of an old way you can get horses used to camels that may work. You could try it. Bonnie, bring a blanket from the shed – one that hasn't been washed.'

'Sure.' She's soon back, and hands a red blanket to Alex. 'Put this on Jago.'

'Actually,' Sully says, 'best to just leave it near him at first so he's got a chance to move away from it and get used to it in his own time. When he can stomach it, put it on him when you're riding him, and take it off afterwards. Might take a while, but he should get used to the smell.'

'And if he sees enough of Ruby it might help, too,' Bonnie says with a grin.

36

Alex thinks about it. Does he want to mess with Jago's head like this?

'That is,' Bonnie adds, 'if you want Ruby and me to go for rides with you. I'd love to see the places around here that you know. I've only been to Rocky Peak so far. That place is so cool – it's like touching the sky up there.'

Alex glances north – Rocky Peak stands on the border between the two properties, only a kay or so away. It would be good to show Bonnie the creek, dry now, and maybe the ruins of his great-great-grandparents' first home. Jago's staring their way and seems more relaxed.

Bonnie doesn't say anything about meeting her mum, and he doesn't ask about her. He feels clammy when people ask how his dad is. 'I'd better be getting back,' he says, 'and take Jago home.'

'Not before you've met me properly,' the old man says. He's returning to the yards, leading the calf.

Alex is surprised at what good ears he has.

'Sorry, Pop,' Bonnie says. 'Pop's my great-grandfather. He's Sully's grandpop.'

Alex looks at him in respect. 'It's good to meet you, um . . .' And it's like Bonnie understands he doesn't know how to address him.

'You can call him Pop, can't he, Pop?'

'Certainly.'

Pop's wearing baggy pants and a very long shirt; Bonnie explains they're traditional Afghan clothes. 'It's called a shalwar qameez.' It will take Alex a while before he'll be able to rattle that off like Bonnie. 'The old camel drivers used to wear them, and Pop still finds it the most comfortable outfit to wear.'

Turns out Pop is as bright as a button, as Alex's nan would say. He can remember everything, even poems. He quotes one for Alex like a storyteller, his bleary eyes shining. Alex is not used to someone suddenly performing a poem, but he is unexpectedly moved as he savours the last line: 'Only from the heart can you touch the sky.' Touch the sky. That's what Bonnie said, too. Bet she got it from Pop. It makes him think of the times when his dad showed him the constellations at night near the ghost gum. Pointing up at them was like touching the sky.

'My great-grandfather taught me that.' Pop sounds proud. 'He was the son of one of the first camel drivers who came to South Australia from Afghanistan with the camels. His father helped the explorers, then he did the same when he was older. But he didn't stop there. He made a business out of camels. By the time I was born my grandfather had taken it over, but the trucks came and there was no more use for camels. They were let loose in the desert.'

Bonnie cut in. 'That's also why Sully trains feral camels – they don't need to all be culled. Pop said his family loved their camels so much they couldn't shoot them.'

'Yes,' Pop says. 'It was a sad time – I was a boy but I remember the tears in the eyes of my great-grandfather and grandfather.'

'Pop knows the songs and stories because they lived with his great-grandfather up near Farina when he was a kid.'

'I never met my great-grandmother, but I heard the stories about her,' Pop says, 'how beautiful she was and how my great-grandfather won her hand in marriage through building a successful camel business trekking to Perth and back.'

'What was your great-grandfather's name?' Alex asks.

'Taj Saleh.'

Alex nods at the interesting name.

'Taj means crown. My great-grandmother always said he was the crown of her life.' Pop smiles. 'My great-grandfather had loved her since he was a boy – they grew up together on the camel station at Beltana.'

Sully chuckles. 'Don't chew the boy's ears off, Pop. He mightn't be interested.'

'Nah, it's all good.' Alex likes family stories – he's been told plenty about his family too. How his dad's ancestors emigrated from Scotland and his mum's from Cornwall to work the Burra Mine, then the Moonta one before they became farmers settling here. But his mum's parents died when he was young. What a treasure Bonnie has.

Sully looks at the sky and stops his work. 'I'll take you home, Alex. About time I said hello to the neighbours.'

'Mum won't be home yet. She cooks for the pub in town on Friday nights.' Alex doesn't feel like mentioning his dad. 'I'll walk over to Jago and ride him home the way I came.'

'Righto, another time.'

'I'll walk with you to Jago,' Bonnie says. 'I'll just get a big airtight can to put the blanket in so Jago can't smell it.'

'Sure.'

On the way across the paddock, Bonnie says, 'Can I come to your place another time? I want to see your dog that waits for you to come home.'

'Tangi?'

She looks puzzled. 'That her name?'

Alex grins. 'Cornish. It means fire dog.' It's out before he realises he'll need to explain.

Bonnie's eyes gleam. 'That is a wonderful name. Why did you—?'

Alex's face shuts down, and she stops mid-sentence. 'Sorry, I didn't mean to pry.'

He breathes out in relief. 'It's okay.' But he doesn't want to explain the reason for Tangi's name right now. Nor does Bonnie press him. Her eyes are kind as she looks at him, like she knows how he feels.

Five

‖‖‖

Alex wakes up and stretches. Saturday mornings are good – he doesn't have to get up early to catch the bus. Interesting at Bonnie's place yesterday, seeing the camels. Jago was annoying racing off like that, though. When Alex told him off on the way home, Jago just snorted. Alex can't wait to see if their idea of a camel blanket will help his horse get used to camels. He throws the covers back and pulls on his jeans and shirt.

Jago nearly turns feral when Alex first puts the camel blanket on a fence near him, even though he places it as far away as possible from where Jago eats.

Jago still knows it's there – his eyes show their whites as if Alex is torturing him. Tangi sniffs the blanket and barks once, like, *What are you scared of, you silly duffer?*

Alex squats and holds her head in his hands. 'You are a special girl, you know that, don't you, Tangi?' He tickles behind her ears, smooths the tan fur on either side of her muzzle, strokes her black head and back. 'I'm counting on you to show Jago not to be afraid. You're older than he is.' She steadies her feet and looks him in the eyes. He smiles right back into her orange ones. 'You guys are my lifeline, don't forget.'

Jago nickers, but Tangi raises her snout higher and stares at Alex. He rests his forehead on hers. 'I'm so thankful to have you. What would I do otherwise?'

Tangi yips like she knows what he means, but Jago chomps his hay.

'Oh, there you are, Alexander.' It's his mum.

'Hey.' Alex stands up. He didn't get to talk to her much last night when she came in late. 'It was good next door yesterday – Bonnie's dad retrains feral camels.'

'That the new girl?' She picks up a broom while Alex brings Jago over to the shed to brush him.

'Yeah. Bonnie. The camels are pets. I can't believe they were feral like brumbies, and now they're as tame as alpacas. You could meet Sully and his grandfather. They're so interesting.'

His mum looks up. 'And when would I have time to do that?'

The guilt smacks him in the chest. He needs to do more. Which he doesn't mind, but he can't do more until he's finished studying. He's looking forward to that.

Mum smiles then and ruffles his hair. 'Pity your dad didn't grow up here like you, learning to cope with this environment—' Her smile disappears as quickly as her words.

'What do you mean, Mum?'

'Sorry, Alexander, I didn't mean to say that. It was unfair. It's just that growing up down south didn't

42

prepare him for the tough weather up here.' She puts the broom back and gives him a quick hug. 'I need you to help me this morning since Tom's not feeling well enough to work with the sheep. A few of them have got out of the north-eastern paddock and we need to fix the fence. After we've caught the sheep.'

Alex is stronger than his mum now. It used to be Dad or her doing the work and he'd be holding stuff. Now he gets to do the work and she holds the tools.

He takes her lead and doesn't pursue the conversation about his dad, but his head is spinning. It's the first comment she's made about his dad for ages.

He helps Mum put the tools in the back of the ute, Tangi jumps onto the tray, and he drives to the paddock. They only need to walk up one side of the paddock before they find the wool on the barbed wire. 'They came through here, Mum.'

'They've made a mess of the fence.'

'How many got through?' They scan the paddock – the mob of sheep huddle together, searching for shoots on the ground. You'd think they'd give up hope.

His mother shades her eyes, surveying them. 'We're lucky they didn't all follow the renegades. Maybe only a few did. Take Tangi and the ute and bring them back. I'll get started here.'

Alex throws himself into the driver's seat. He'll try to be quick – his mum can do fencing, but she'll need his pair of hands. He drives back through the gate, shuts it and checks the next paddock, where his mum must have seen the runaway sheep. A whirly-whirly spirals in front of him as it moves to the south, throwing dust onto the windscreen. At first he can't see a thing. Surely the sheep haven't pushed through another fence thinking they were going home?

He drives around the fence line – nothing. Maybe they got through to another paddock. This could take all day. Then he notices black kites circling above the centre of the paddock. Tangi barks from the tray.

As Alex drives over to some bushes, the birds glide higher. Kites usually mean a dead body; their feeding habits help farmers by cleaning up carcasses. Tangi jumps off and sniffs the ground and the bushes, then races further away. Alex follows her. When he drives up over a rise, Tangi is sitting still with an *I found it* stance. Lying in front of her is a sheep.

Alex gets out of the ute. It's mauled and half-eaten. What would have done this? Foxes only take lambs; they don't attack fully grown sheep. He tries not to think about the monster dog he saw at Rocky Peak. He still hasn't told his parents about that.

He hears a faint mewling and heads towards the sound. Behind some saltbush he finds a live ewe, a bit skittish as he approaches, but the tiny cry is coming from the bush. 'Oh, hello.' He picks up a lamb and cradles it as he walks back to the ute. It's shaking and probably hungry. He lays it on the floor of the cabin and wraps a rag around it.

He pushes the ewe up onto the ute tray until she scrambles aboard. Tangi jumps up with her and lies flat in the opposite corner so as not to spook her. Alex glows with pride – he hardly ever has to tell Tangi what to do.

When he reaches his mum, she looks surprised. 'Only one?'

Alex brings out the lamb. His mum frowns. 'Maybe the lamb got through and the mother went after her?'

'I don't think that's the mother of the lamb.'

She inspects the sheep. 'Oh, I see, this one hasn't lambed yet.'

'There's a dead sheep, probably the mother. She's been mauled, half-eaten.'

His mum blows out a breath. 'Must be wild dogs.'

'Could a feral dog do that?'

She nods. 'A big hungry one that can't find feed or water.'

'Guess we haven't seen many rabbits lately.'

'Not enough feed for rabbits, so that brings the feral animals closer to properties.'

'Mum, there's something I've been wanting to tell you. I couldn't tell Dad because he would worry and I was going to tell you, but I thought you were too tired—'

His mum cuts in, her voice terse. 'What is it?'

'I saw a feral dog on Rocky Peak last Thursday after school. It tried to go Jago.' He doesn't say it had its eye on him as well once he was on the ground. No need to get her too worried.

His mother sighs. 'I'll find out if anyone else has had trouble. We'll have to keep a close eye on the sheep. We'll put this mob in the paddock closest to the sheds.'

'Shall we move them now?'

'Let's fix the fence first. Then we'll pick up the dead one so it doesn't bring the dog back.'

'I'm sorry, Mum. If I'd told you earlier, maybe we wouldn't have lost the sheep.'

'You mustn't blame yourself, Alexander. It could have happened anyway.'

Then she mumbles under her breath, though Alex hears, 'Is there any end to the trouble this drought's still causing?'

Alex makes a mental note to check his chook shed is feral dog–proof.

He keeps the lamb with him and after putting the ute back in the shed, he drives the quad bike out to move the sheep, the lamb cradled in his lap and Tangi on the back. She's a great help – doesn't wind them up like a motorbike or helicopter would. She even gives the lamb a comforting lick. Not for the first time, Alex wishes dogs lived longer than they do. He whistles like his dad used to, and Tangi jumps off and keeps the mob following Alex. She circles the mob from the back, then weaves side to side to pick up stragglers. He grins. Kelpies always want to herd the animals towards their alpha – in this case, him. She's still a great muster dog.

He creeps the bike to the new paddock so the sheep are not rushed. Once they're settled, Alex puts the orphaned lamb by a new mum with one lamb, pushing the orphan up to the ewe's teats. She doesn't object, but he knows he'll need to check them next morning. She might get tired of two lambs feeding.

When he returns the bike to the shed, he checks the wire walls of his chook shed. When his dad helped him build it, they dug a half-metre trench all around the foundation and filled it with cement. 'That should stop the foxes from digging their way in under it,' his dad said. There are no breaks in the wire, so the dog or fox hasn't come this close.

Alex has a shower while his mum sets up her laptop in the lounge room to Zoom with Lily and their grandparents. He hopes the satellite dish lasts the distance this time. A month ago, there was a strong wind and they had Buckley's chance of finishing their session using video. Afterwards he and his mum spent an hour sweeping the dust out of the house.

Grandad and Nan are already on screen when Alex walks in, his hair still wet. Alex sits by his dad and stares at his grandad. His hair's grey and he looks like Dad probably will in twenty-five years' time. Though lately Dad's been looking older, haggard. Nan's eyes light up when she sees Alex. It's no secret that he also looks like his dad.

Lily starts the ball rolling. She seems different, more mature; it must be because she's wearing her hair up on her head, light brown like their mum's. Alex's is dark, like his dad's and grandad's used to be. Dad leans forward to hear. 'So, there's the PE camp coming up on the weekend, Mum. Outdoor sport, kayaking and stuff – we're going to the Yorke Peninsula—'

'You'll be almost halfway up to us,' Mum says. She forgets to watch for the yellow square that shows who's talking and drowns out the rest of Lily's sentence.

'—can you send the permission form by email, please. Or I can't go and I really want to.' By Lily's tone Alex can tell she has sent it before.

There's a pause this time before Mum says, 'Of course, sorry I didn't see it.' She doesn't spend much time on the laptop – it's mainly for farm bills. She likes calling Lily, but you have to be on the rise behind the house near the ghost gum for that to work best. They can't afford a phone tower like the one in town or on bigger stations.

Grandad's quiet, like Dad, but Nan asks, 'How's school, Alexander?'

'Um, all good, Nan. There's a new girl in our class, Bonnie. Her family's running camels.' At least Bonnie is a safe topic.

'That's nice, Alexander. Where does she live?'

'Next door. Jago doesn't like her camel, though. He streaked for home like a monster was after him.'

Grandad laughs. They had horses on their farm near Clare before they retired to the Adelaide suburbs. 'You'll have fun, Alex, trying to get him used to the camel smell. He's young yet, so it may be worth a try.'

'What would you do, Grandad?'

'Ease him into it. Do it gradually. The early explorers had trouble because they would start on an expedition with both horses and camels without spending time getting the horses used to camels. It will take time, but it is possible.'

'How would I start?'

'Take him over there, but tether him not far away from them and keep the rope long. When he realises they're not going to attack him, he'll calm down. Next time, tether him a bit closer or shorten the rope. Just a step at a time.'

'Sounds like it could take months.'

'Maybe, or it might be just weeks. Let me know how you go.'

Then Alex's dad speaks up. 'Camels aren't a good idea. There shouldn't be a camel farm this far south.'

There's a silence. Mum looks happy that Dad said anything at all. But Alex doesn't agree with him about the camels.

Eventually, his mum says, 'We found a dead sheep today. We think a wild dog . . .' She glances at Dad, but he stays quiet. At times it's like he's not listening, and then he can surprise you. 'The drought is making things difficult enough without feral animals getting at our stock.'

Then suddenly Dad clears his throat. 'When are you coming home, Lily? You've left your brother to do all the work.' It doesn't come out right, not like when he says he misses her.

Lily frowns. 'We can't come until the end of term. It's too far for a return visit on a weekend.' She glances at Nan and Grandad.

Alex notices Nan can't keep her eyes off him. He's their only grandson, and she probably can't wait until he lives with them in Adelaide like Lily. He hopes she doesn't ask about it today. One day, he'll need to tell them it's not happening. He's not leaving Spring Park!

Six

||||||||||||||||||||||||||||||||||||||||||||||||||||||||||||||||||||||

Monday morning comes around all too soon. Alex enjoys heading into school with Harry and Bonnie, but he hopes his mum is having a good day with Dad.

On the bus, Bonnie can't wait to tell Alex her news. Her eagerness makes him smile. 'Guess what? Dad found a roadkill kangaroo. It didn't look big enough to be a male, so he drove slower to make sure. He always checks if he thinks it's a female.' Alex can guess what she'll say next, but he lets her tell the story. 'He noticed her belly moving, but she was as dead as.'

Bonnie checks if he's tracking with her, and he nods to keep her going. 'A joey!' Then her excitement fades. 'Trouble is, all the teats we have are for baby camels. I've been feeding it with a tea towel soaked in milk for it to suck like a teat, but I can tell it's still hungry. I can't sit there all day.'

'I can bring over a teat for feeding newborn lambs.' He brought up a joey once. Let it go when it was big enough to jump fences. 'We have a lone lamb at the moment, but I'm hoping a new mother will keep feeding it. They were still together early this morning.'

'Why a lone lamb?'

Alex hesitates. 'We lost a sheep on the weekend. Found it mauled. There are feral dogs around.'

Bonnie seems to cope with this information. 'I'd like to see your lambs. Why don't you get off the bus with me this arvo, and we'll take you home. I can help with your jobs.'

She certainly livens him up. Alex hopes his parents don't mind him spending time with Bonnie or think he'll shirk his chores with her around. 'What if I ride Jago over, bring the teat and bottle?'

She stares at him, lost for words. 'Are you sure? What about Jago and the camels?'

'My grandad says he just has to get used to them.'

Bonnie's smile is wide. 'You'll be over a lot then.'

After school, Alex asks his mum if she'll be fine with Dad if he visits Bonnie. 'Of course, Alexander.' She smiles, and he races off to saddle up Jago.

'Wish I could tell you not to be frightened, Jago, but you've got to work it out yourself.' He turns to Tangi. 'Stay here, Tangi. If you ride with me, Jago might play up again, and it's too far for you to walk home.' She sits on her haunches and only whines once. Alex kneels and strokes the tan stripes on her cheeks. 'You're a good girl.'

Fortunately, there are no camels in the first paddock they cross on Bonnie's place. He heads for the house, where Bonnie meets him. Some camels are in the yards that Sully was working on last time.

Bonnie sees him checking out the new yards as he dismounts. 'Dad's got more to build before he brings in a new load of desert camels. He's still training this mob before he lets them loose in the paddock.'

'Can I tether Jago here by the house? Will your mum mind?'

'She won't mind. Put him here by the clothesline. That way he can see the camels, yet they're too far away to be a threat.'

'I hope he follows your line of thinking.' Alex scans the distance between the house and the camel yards. There are a few trees Jago could gradually progress to. 'Okay. Let's try this.' He ties his rope to the reins so Jago can back up, but not so far that he's in Bonnie's backyard.

Jago pricks his ears forward.

'He can see them.'

'He can smell them, too.' Bonnie chuckles.

Jago shifts his feet and backs up as far as the rope will allow. Then he stands still. Watches. Blows out a few times, then snorts. Lifts his head up and down twice. Mostly he just keeps watching the camels hanging around the yards.

'I think he'll be all right,' Alex says. 'Thought he'd make more of a fuss.'

'Maybe the camel blanket has helped already?'

'It's early days,' Alex murmurs, watching Jago. 'We'll see what happens when I go to the yards.'

First, Bonnie shows him the joey in the backyard. It's a grey. He picks it up and it dives headfirst down his shirt. 'Hey! Ow, that scratches.' The joey turns and pokes her head out of the top of Alex's shirt. 'When I had a joey it was always trying to get down my jumper. This one might need a sack to disappear in. Dad nailed one on the side of the veranda for ours.'

'That's a good idea.'

Alex hands over the bottle and Bonnie runs inside to warm up milk. When she returns with it, the joey pulls on it as if she's never had a feed in her life.

'Incredible,' Bonnie says. 'That sure works a treat.' When the bottle is finished, she helps drag the joey out of Alex's shirt and puts her on the ground.

'I'll check on Jago,' he says. He pats him and rubs his neck. 'You have to be brave, Jago.' When Alex walks away from him towards the rails, Jago snorts and rolls up his lip like, *Hey, you're not leaving me here by myself?* But Alex is determined not to go back. Bonnie is right behind him.

'G'day, Alex,' Sully says. He seems to be teaching a young camel to sit. Pop's there too, supervising by the look of it. 'I see you've brought your horse.'

'Yeah – my grandad said I could try to get him used to your camels gradual-like.'

'That can work, but it's slower. If you're a patient guy, it'll be okay.'

Alex nods. 'This camel is cute.'

Bonnie agrees. 'Really cute, but if we don't train them when they get to this age, like three, they won't be respectful pets. So Sully teaches them to sit. Can't ride them or get them to carry things if they won't sit on command. They'd end up just being a paddock pet.'

Alex can see the sense of that. Like training horses to take the bit, the bridle, the saddle. Then he remembers the dead sheep. 'Have you seen any feral dogs?'

Sully shakes his head. 'Wouldn't get any here.'

'Why's that?'

'They won't come near camels.'

'Like Jago?'

'Nup – they know camels can kick. The camels chase off foxes and wild dogs. It's like having a giant alpaca in the paddock.'

'What if we lent Alex a camel,' Bonnie says, 'to protect their sheep?'

Sully says, 'Hoosta,' and the young camel stands again. He regards Alex. 'I don't mind, but you'll need two. Camels pine if left on their own – they need each other to learn things or they get lonely.'

'Would they step on the lambs?' Alex says. Even the young camels' feet are huge. 'A few dropped recently.'

'Nup, these are gentle giants. People only get a problem with pet camels if they haven't trained them and let them think they're the boss. Boundaries need to be set for their behaviour, like any other animal.' Alex suspects not everyone around here would agree that camels are gentle giants.

Sully says, 'Hoosta,' again and, as he holds the nose rope, the young camel folds his front legs and sinks to the ground, not without a few groans.

Alex watches the camel sitting on the ground. *Guess*

horses are the same. If his dad hadn't shown him how to train Jago, he wouldn't be able to do a thing with him now he's three years old. Pity that training didn't involve getting used to camels. He glances back at Jago. He's still as far away as the rope will allow, but he's not whinnying or shuffling his feet, just intently watching on high alert, his ears stretched forward as if on invisible strings.

'I'll ask Mum and Dad about the camels. Thanks.' After Dad's comment on Zoom, Alex is certain he won't agree. He isn't sure what his mum will say, either, which reminds him of Bonnie answering for her mother so confidently earlier. How did she know what her mum would think?

'There's Ruby's mother, Emmie. We named her after Pop's Scottish great-grandmother Emmeline,' Bonnie says as a camel ambles over to the yards. 'She's been in the paddock. She's gorgeous, but we couldn't lend her to you – Ruby still needs her for learning how to be a camel.'

That makes sense too. Camels with sheep – it's a new idea for their family. He wonders what his grandad will make of it. Riding Jago back after he's said goodbye to the Salehs, he wonders how he can raise the idea of camels with his mum. He'll have to pick the right moment.

At home he finishes his chores and comes in for dinner. His dad is still in the lounge room and his mum is already serving up the veggies and lamb chops. She makes great gravy with rosemary.

He goes into the lounge room where the news is on silent. 'Hey Dad, let's have tea.' His dad doesn't respond. 'It's your favourite – lamb chops and gravy.'

His mum comes to help, and between them they get Dad on his feet. 'You have to eat, Tom, keep up your strength.' It will be one of those nights when Alex will need to cut up his dad's food to ensure he eats it. What a way to finish a great afternoon with Bonnie.

Seven

||||||||||||||||||||||||||||||||||||||||||||||||||||||||||||||||||||||||||||||||||||||||

Alex wakes up hearing howling. Is he dreaming? Then snarling – it sounds too close. Tangi's barking, and he can hear the clang of her pulling on the chain. She sounds frantic. Then he hears flapping, squawking. *His chickens!* His mum shouts. Or is it a scream?

He pulls on his jacket and races out to the veranda. Sounds like Jago is kicking the shed wall.

'Mum?' She's out by the chook shed in her dressing-gown, brandishing a rake. 'Get going!' she screams. 'Get out of it!'

What's going on? Then he sees it – a rangy dog, much bigger than Tangi, unkempt, grey. Is it the same one he saw on Rocky Peak? Looks like it. Usually feral animals will run when challenged, but this one backs up, circles, advances again. What's made it so aggressive? It's all mouth and teeth, one big hungry snarl.

His mum sees him. 'Get back inside, Alexander. I can handle this.'

It doesn't look like she's handling it. The dog is edging closer to her. She's standing between it and the chooks, and by now the dog can't bear the frenzy and smell of the flapping and squawking coming from the shed. It will go his mum for sure. What can he do?

The gun. They have a .22 rifle. But he doesn't know where the key to the gun cupboard is. Only licenced people are allowed that information. He'll have to wake up Dad. He ducks inside to the main bedroom and shakes his dad awake.

'Wh-wh the madder?'

'Dad, you have to help Mum. There's a feral dog trying to get the chooks.'

For a moment he thinks his dad is going to roll over again, but he stirs himself. Sits on the side of the bed. 'Where's the key to the gun cupboard? Dad?'

His dad stands, and Alex grabs his dressing-gown and puts it on him. Tangi hasn't stopped barking. What if the feral dog goes for her? She's on the chain and won't be able to defend herself.

They walk to the office, not fast enough for Alex. 'We have to hurry!'

His father touches the desk, then the second drawer. 'It's in a tin.'

Alex yanks open the drawer and scrabbles for the tin, finds it at the back, rips it open. He holds the key out to his dad, but knows he won't be able to use it. In his haste, even Alex struggles to get it in the keyhole of the steel cupboard. He has never been allowed to touch the gun, and he shouldn't be doing this. Even his dad has never used it since the fire.

He brings the gun to his dad. Dad, wider awake now, walks over to the cupboard and reaches for a small box from the top. Alex breathes a sigh of relief – he may not have found the bullets in time by himself. His father pulls the barrel down and inserts one bullet. Snaps it shut. Puts another in his pocket.

Alex leads him out to the veranda. Will his dad be able to shoot? His mum's still screaming at the dog, amid Tangi's frenzied barking. Alex suspects the wild dog is hungry, but hunger won't overcome fear. They need to frighten it off, but it doesn't seem to be easily frightened.

His dad raises the gun, but the light's not good and he hesitates.

His mum sees them. 'Tom, go back to bed, I'm fine.'

Dad lowers the gun. Alex takes it from him and runs it to his mum. 'You have to shoot it, Mum.'

She takes it – surely she knows Dad isn't capable. Alex takes over the rake and brandishes it at the dog. He moves closer.

The dog stops snarling. It sits and stares at them, brazen as a fox. The chooks squawk. Sounds like they're trying to fly the coop. The dog steps forward.

Alex shouts, 'Shoot it, Mum. It'll go ya!' There'll be no time to get the second bullet off Dad, to frighten it off. She'll have to shoot to kill. He growls at the dog in a voice so like his dad's he scares himself. 'Get out of it!'

His mum has the gun trained on the dog, and right then it springs.

'Mum!'

She pulls the trigger.

The dog flops to the ground, one huge paw on her slipper.

She staggers back, and Alex puts an arm around her.

'You're a good shot, Mum.' His voice comes out shaky. He glances at the veranda, but his dad's gone.

'My brother taught me.' Then she bursts into tears.

Alex wraps his arms around her and holds her like he's seen his dad do. She pulls a tissue out of her dressing-gown pocket.

'I didn't want to shoot it – it was just hungry.'

Alex gives her a wobbly grin. 'And you were going to get rid of that beast with a rake?'

She leans against him. 'It worked with Tangi when she was young.'

'Tangi is a purebred kelpie, Mum. A fly swat would have worked on her.' Tangi barks once, like, *watch what you're saying.*

'Lock the gun in the cupboard, Alexander. I'll hide the key. Let's hope we don't have to use it ever again.'

'What would Dad have done if he was well?' Alex asks softly.

She sighs. 'He would have shot the dog to save me and the chooks.'

They walk up the steps to the veranda, and inside. Dad is by the lounge-room window; he must have seen it all. Tears are running down his face. 'I'm so sorry, Rach.'

Alex and Mum put their arms around him as he sobs. 'I wanted to help.'

'Shhh,' Mum says. 'It's over now.'

But Alex feels the weight of his dad's despair and powerlessness. Will he ever again be the strong man he used to be? Dad sags in their hug and they help him to bed.

Eight

||||||||||||||||||||||||||||||||||||||||||||||||||||||||||||||||||||||||||||||||

'Dad? Breakfast.'

There are no answering shuffles or sounds. Alex is nervous to see what Dad is like after last night. His dad's never wide awake early in the day, but this morning he won't even come to the table. Alex makes scrambled eggs and takes it on a tray to him in bed.

His mum comes out to the kitchen to join him after a shower. She has dark shadows around her eyes. At first Alex gets a shock, as that's how his dad's eyes look lately. 'I'm fine,' his mum says, 'just tired. Your dad didn't sleep well.'

'Was it having to get the gun?'

She nods. 'Had to reassure him we weren't killing more sheep. He was also upset because he couldn't bring himself to use the gun.'

Then she looks up at Alex. 'That was too close last night.'

Maybe now is the time.

Alex lets out a quiet breath. 'You know Bonnie's

family runs camels? They say the camels are good in a paddock to protect other animals, like alpacas are.'

She frowns at him. 'Camels can keep dogs away?'

Alex nods. 'They can kick.' Then he adds, 'If we did it, would Dad understand?'

'I don't know.' She rolls her hair and secures it on top of her head. 'Last night, once he knew it wasn't sheep dying, he felt better – even said he'd get more help. He'll ask his counsellor about meds. He has his moments. It's just this morning he's . . . slumped again.'

She slumps too, and Alex can't stop his eyes from tearing up. He so wants good moments to become the norm. For his dad to be up at dawn, ready to go, teaching him stuff again, like fencing, driving and mechanics. 'Working together with Dad was great.'

He doesn't realise he's said that aloud until his mum squeezes his hand. 'It will be again, Alexander.'

He wants to ask, *When?* like he's a little kid. 'Some people don't get better,' he says instead. 'That guy west of town couldn't handle losing his property. He died.' Alex can't say how. He doesn't want suicide to be a reality for his family.

His mum wraps her arms around him. 'Your dad has us to love him and remind him to take care of himself. He has his mates, his faith. Please don't worry, Alexander. Your dad is having counselling, and it is helping.'

Just then Tangi barks once and they hear a ute door shut. 'G'day, anyone home?'

Alex rushes to the door. It's Sully. He's in his usual khaki duds and looks a lot like Bear Grylls this morning.

Mum's still in her dressing-gown, but Alex invites him in.

'This is Sully, Mum, from next door. Sully, this is my mum—'

'Rachael,' she cuts in. 'Would you like a coffee? Flat white?'

Sully glances at the coffee machine on the bench. 'I sure would. Thanks. Just popped in to see if everything is okay over here . . .?' He says it as a question.

'Did you hear the shot last night?' Alex asks.

'You betcha. I was out seeing to a calf. It was a still night, breeze coming my way – sound travels.'

'It was a feral dog after the chooks,' Alex says. 'Mum shot it.'

She puts the coffee in front of Sully and sits beside Alex. 'It was a shock. We've never had feral dogs around before.'

'The drought,' is all Sully says. He tastes the coffee. 'Mmm, that's good. You sure know how to make coffee like a cafe.'

She nods. 'Thanks, I've had to learn at the pub. Look, Alex told me about the camels and your kind offer – I need to discuss it with Tom, my husband.'

'No worries.' Sully stands, finishing his coffee. Alex is glad he hasn't stated the obvious: that it'd be a mistake not to have camels with feral dogs around. 'Better get back to work. Pop and I are building a dairy. We're going to milk the camels.' He grins at the look on her face. 'Yep, bet you serve camel steaks at the pub – why not camel cheese or camel milkshakes? Great for people intolerant of cow's milk.' He chuckles. 'People will change their minds about camels one day.' He pauses at the door, his hat in his hand. 'Rachael, let me know if I can help in any way at all.' By the way he says *any*, Alex can tell he means it.

Alex wonders what Sully's heard, while his mum stutters, 'W-we're fine, thanks.'

Alex is quiet on the bus. Harry doesn't jolly him around as he usually might, and neither does Bonnie. Maybe Sully told her about the night Alex had.

He spends the time drawing; his picture turns into a ferocious wolf with long fangs, ready to pounce. Apart from his dad being affected, Alex thinks two feral dogs in a short time are two too many. The aftermath of the shooting and this morning has finally caught up with him.

During lunchbreak Alex and Harry have to empty out the classroom recycling bin on the veranda into the big recycling bins behind the staffroom. Harry says, 'Your mum rang my old man to have a lookout in case we get a feral dog like you did. Must've been scary, eh?'

Alex nods.

Harry changes the subject. 'Look at all this paper. Could make something cool out of it.' He folds a sheet of red paper into a hat and slaps it on Alex's head. 'Aaargh! You look like a pirate, me beauty.' Harry hops around, pretending he has only one leg. He's so wacky Alex can't help laughing.

'You're a galah, Harry.'

Harry cracks up. 'Look who's talking, mate.' Then he says on the way out to the big bins, 'Actually I'm a black cockatoo,' and he gives a rendition of a cockatoo's raucous call.

Harry's bird calls are legendary in the school, and some younger kids hear it and squeal, 'Do it again, Harry. Do it again!'

'I'll teach you to squawk like a galah later.'

Alex grins. What would he do without Harry?

Kris, the pastoral care worker, says, 'G'day,' as he walks past Alex towards the staffroom where his office is. Alex notices Summer is walking beside him. She looks as glum as he felt this morning on the bus. He makes an effort and calls out, 'Hi, Summer.' But she keeps her gaze on the ground.

'Do you know what's up with Summer?' Alex asks Harry.

Harry shrugs. 'She sure looks like a half-sucked peppermint lately. Maybe that's why she picks on us.'

Alex smirks. Harry's sayings are funny.

When they finish with the recycling bins, Harry says, 'Let's play footy.' He runs to get a ball from their class-room and brings it back under his arm. They rush across to the oval – or to be precise, their dusty paddock. There are enough Year Five and Six boys who want to play, then Sophie and Bonnie turn up.

'Sophie and I can play,' Bonnie says.

Some more Year Six girls join them. They have enough players now to have a good game even though they don't have full teams.

Bonnie's fast, and a good mark, but she runs too far with the ball.

'Hey,' Alex calls, 'you're holding the ball.' Bonnie kicks it to Sophie.

Harry shouts to Alex, 'We could make a mixed team.'

Alex thinks it's a good idea. Sophie's a great player. Bonnie's ponytail swishes as she runs with the ball again. 'Kick it,' Alex calls. They'd need to come to training.

Then the bell sounds and all the kids disperse. Bonnie and Sophie run off, laughing.

Harry wipes the sweat off his face with his shirt. 'Ready to do battle this arvo?'

Alex stares at him. 'What's going on?'

'You'll see, you galah.'

Alex laughs. Harry can cheer him up every time with just a roll of his eyes or a few words. It's all about the way he says things.

Alex feels the heavy atmosphere in the classroom as soon as he enters. He's read about it in novels: *you could cut the air with a knife*. He raises his eyebrows at Bonnie as he sits down, but she doesn't react, just looks determined, like she's trying not to retaliate. What a change from the oval.

He glances at the older girls. Sophie looks uncomfortable, but Tara is glaring at Bonnie. Summer's red in the face like she's been on the oval without her hat. She's changed from sad to angry pretty quick. What's happened?

Mr Clarke is setting up the computer to watch a video in STEM. 'Ms Shultz told me you're discussing climate change in geography. This video is about the carbon footprint of a water bottle. We'll look at some scientific implications of that. We're all beginning to realise that it's best not to make new plastic, and instead to recycle the plastic we have.' He starts the video of a scientist talking about how they've worked out that producing a water bottle causes eighty-three grams of carbon to be released into the atmosphere. Factors include the energy needed to transport the bottle, and to turn resins into plastic; even packing, storage, cleaning and filling the bottles contributes to the final footprint. Bonnie's writing notes. A *recycled* water bottle, however, reduces its carbon emission by more than fifty per cent.

Mr Clarke says, 'Write a personal response. Imagine you can do anything and had the money to do so; decide what you'd like to achieve to improve the environment near you. Think about an option, what you'd need and how it would work, and who you'd need to persuade to help get it going. What problem would you like to solve to help your place using science or digital technology or engineering?' Then he adds, 'The response can be creative – a proposal, a letter to the paper and so on.'

Harry whispers to Alex, 'We're going to be flat out like a lizard drinkin'.'

Alex stares at him.

'You know – busy?'

Alex whispers back, 'You're a galah, Harry.'

'Boys.' Mr Clarke's tone silences them.

Alex thinks about the movie he saw of William, a

thirteen-year-old boy in Malawi building a windmill from scrap metal and saving his village from famine during a drought. William used library books to work out how to engineer it. Alex'd like to do something like that. A way to make rain would be helpful.

Bonnie's super quiet after the video, just doing her task as are the others. It all comes out when Mr Clarke asks a few people to read a paragraph of their response.

Tara starts. 'I've written a letter to the editor. *I would like to bring to your attention a worrying situation in our district. There has been an influx of feral camels on a camel farm. We all know how much damage they have caused to stations up north, breaking down fences. Now our water supplies, stock and any vegetation we have left will not be safe with camels around. They are bad for the environment, ferocious, growl like bears and even eat lambs—*'

At this point Mr Clarke stops her. 'Two things, Tara. Firstly, you need to do research before writing a factual piece for a newspaper. Camels were herbivores the last time I checked. And how did the video about water bottles make you think of camels?'

Tara retorts, 'I'm worried about the lack of water in our district in the drought. Climate change is bad enough as it is without having camels in the mix drinking all our water.'

Everyone except Summer and Bonnie stare at her. How can she blame climate change on camels? Cows maybe, but *camels*?

Alex admires Bonnie's self-control. If anyone was bagging Jago and said he was ferocious, ate lambs and contributed to climate change, he'd be telling them where to get off. But Bonnie just sits there, not defending herself, with that look of controlled resolve. It makes her seem more mature than Tara, who's clearly just having a dig at Bonnie. Alex has to take a deep breath to calm down.

Sophie has written an interesting report of the things her grandmother is teaching her about bush tucker, and a story about how the moon got in the sky. 'My gran says I must write everything down that she teaches me about our Adnyamathanha culture so I can pass it on to my kids and they can keep looking after our environment here, just like my ancestors have for thousands of years. So my ideal project would be making a photo book of all she's teaching me.'

'I'm sure that will be a worthy project, Sophie. Well done.'

'Summer?' Mr Clarke raises his eyebrows.

Alex glances at her. Summer looks uncomfortable, even sad again like at lunchtime. 'Sorry, I couldn't think of anything that would work.'

Harry's written a limerick about the drought and lack of water and how to fix it, but Mr Clarke stops him before he finishes. 'Thanks, I think we get the drift,' he says. He sounds tired.

So that's what must have happened back in the classroom while they were on the oval. Some of the girls were bagging Bonnie and her camels and she must have heard them as she and Sophie came back in. Alex frowns at Tara.

On the bus, Harry is philosophical about it. 'Don't take any notice of those girls, Bonnie.' He doesn't say he disagrees with them, just that they went too far. 'You can hang around with us.'

Bonnie smiles. 'Thanks, guys. Then she surprises them. 'My mum says it's no business of mine what other people think of me.'

Alex can't think of anything to top that.

Nine

||||||||||||||||||||||||||||||||||||||||||||||||||||||||||||||||||||||||||||||

It's Saturday morning again and Alex enjoys a breather. He reads a chapter of *The Hobbit* before his mum comes in. 'Alexander, after the feed run, could you check the sheep are okay?'

Alex drives the ute into the closest paddock. The sheep are restless, and Tangi barks a few times. Alex drums his fingers on the steering wheel. One lot runs from one corner to the other when he drives the ute around the paddock. Usually they stay in one spot, or chase him if he has hay, not run away like this.

He gets out to have a better look. Everything seems fine, but he's unnerved. Tangi is on edge too. Lanky stands apart from the others as usual. She trots up and playfully butts him. 'Hey, Lanky, you worked out you're a sheep yet?' She follows him to the ute and all the way to the gate, bleating. 'Bye, Lanky.'

In another paddock the sheep are crouched together under the trees. Sheep get nervous easily. Right now, they seem frightened. They disperse as soon as he drives past them down to the other end of the paddock where they were the last time he came. That's where he sees it.

He jumps out of the ute. Tangi hits the ground before him and they both run to the mound of wool on the ground. He hopes it's just asleep, but he knows better. Tangi is there first, sniffing the sheep then sitting upright for Alex to inspect her work.

'Good finding, Tangi.' He kicks the dirt. They can't afford to lose sheep like this. It has been mauled like the other ewe. He was hoping the feral dog his mum killed was the only one. He surveys the next paddock, then the horizon. How many are out there? He whistles for Tangi to jump onto the tray and drives as fast as he's allowed to the sheds.

His mum's in the kitchen drinking coffee when he rushes in.

She looks up. 'Alexander? What's wrong?'

'We have to move the sheep in the north paddock. There's another dead one.'

She frowns. 'Like before?'

'Same.'

'So there's another dog . . .' Her voice trails away.

'Mum, we need those camels.'

'Tom—' Then she stops to think. 'What if a camel kicks a sheep? They are feral, after all, and so much bigger than alpacas. What if the sheep share Jago's fear of them? What if we end up beholden to Bonnie's family somehow? Their Afghan culture is so different—'

Alex can't believe what he's hearing. 'Mum, they're as Aussie as we are. Do we still call ourselves Cornish?'

She gives a wry grin. 'Sorry, I can't believe I said that. Look, I have to get it past your dad. At the moment he's not himself, not thinking straight.' She glances at Alex.

'Can we do it without him knowing, Mum? He's hardly ever out in the paddocks now. We have to do *something*.' Alex's voice is rising, but he stops at the anguished look on his mum's face and goes to her. 'I'm sorry, Mum. I didn't mean to tell you what to do.'

'Alexander, I understand you're worried, but we'll get through this.'

He nods, even though he's thinking there's a feral dog's banquet in the paddocks. What if Lanky gets taken? She's always so unafraid and apart from the others.

His mother hugs him. 'Let's shift the sheep, Alexander. I'll deal with Tom.'

Sully and Bonnie come over after lunch. Bonnie gives her usual sunny smile, and Alex introduces her. 'Mum, this is Bonnie.'

'Hello, Bonnie, I've heard a lot about you.' Alex can tell his mum is warming to Bonnie right away. Who wouldn't, except for those two girls at school.

Sully walks in after Bonnie. 'Rachael.' He tips his hat. 'G'day.'

She shakes his hand. 'Thanks for coming over. It's about the camels.' She pauses. 'Tom isn't keen,' she gives an apologetic smile, 'but Alexander is.'

Alex wonders where his dad is and what Mum has said to him. She won't want their family to be seen as a charity case, and her next words prove it. 'We can pay for them to be here,' she says firmly.

Sully won't have a bar of it. 'You'll be feeding them.' He sounds incredulous.

'Right,' she says, 'they'll be eating our saltbush and weeds. Either way I look at it, as long as your camels don't kill our sheep, we're the ones better off.'

'You'll be giving them a change of eating space. That helps me too.'

Rachael regards Sully dubiously. Alex can almost tell what she's thinking now – what if the camels get left there when she doesn't need them anymore and the weeds run out, as if that would ever happen. Then she'd need to buy in more hay. Alex is sure if anything like that happened Sully would supply feed.

'It'll be okay, Mum,' Alex says quietly.

Not once has Sully asked where Tom is or what he thinks about the camels. That says a lot. Sully is a guy they can trust, he's sure of it.

Mum sighs. 'All right. When will they come?'

Sully tips his chin at Bonnie. She says, 'Alex and I can bring them over Rocky Peak this arvo if you like.'

Alex watches his mum's eyebrows rise. 'Are you happy about that, Alexander?'

'Absolutely.'

'We hope this does two things for you,' Sully says. 'One, save your sheep and two, get Jago so used to camels that Bonnie and Alex can go for a ride together.'

He makes it sound like Alex and his mum are doing the Salehs a favour, not the other way round, and his mum loosens up and smiles wider at him. Alex hasn't seen her smile so openly for a long time. Even her green eyes crinkle at the corners. It makes Alex relax too.

'So do they really only eat weeds?' she says.

Sully grins. 'They'll eat whatever's going, but they like saltbush and anything thorny. They're not fond of green grass. Too insipid.'

'They'll be fine here, then,' his mum says. Is she actually cracking a joke?

Sully puts his hat on. 'See you round then, Rachael.'

Bonnie gives Alex a wink. 'See ya.'

Later that afternoon Alex goes to the house paddock and gives a whistle. Jago lifts his head. 'C'mon, boy. Let's ride.' Tangi lopes over. 'Tangi, stay home. We're bringing camels and I'm not sure how it will go.'

Jago gives a whinny and trots over. Alex is glad his horse is well trained. He usually does what he's told, except when he can smell camel. Alex grimaces. He hopes Jago doesn't disgrace himself at Bonnie's place this time. He'll have to come back first in line, and Bonnie will probably ride Ruby and lead the other camels.

It works out as he expects. After he deposits Jago by the house, his rope tied a metre shorter than the last time, Alex walks over to the yards where Bonnie and Sully are. Pop, too. Gertrude the kisser is one camel they choose. Also Asmaan, a gelding, a lighter colour than Gertrude or Ruby.

'Asmaan is an interesting name,' Alex says. 'What's it mean?' By now he knows Bonnie's family doesn't name anything without thinking about it.

'Heaven,' Bonnie says. 'When he was born he was as pale as the sky that day, overcast. It looked like rain.'

'Did it rain?'

She shook her head. 'We still named him Asmaan.' She stretches out the 'a' sound in the middle of his name.

Sully says, 'Good to see ya, mate,' as if he hasn't already seen him today. It makes Alex feel warm. Pop salutes him.

'Just so the camels don't end up paddock camels, you may as well learn how to put a saddle on – and to do that you have to make them sit.' Alex remembers from the last time.

'Tug the rope and say *hoosta!*'

'Does saying *hoosta* help?'

'Sure does. These camels are as clever as dogs. But they need to know who's boss. Bond with them and train them well, and they'll sit and stand when you want them to.'

Sounds a lot like training muster dogs like Tangi. 'Could I try?' Alex asks.

'Sure.' Sully gives him Gertrude's rope.

'Hoosta!' Alex says as he tugs the rope. Gertrude groans a lot and is probably telling him he's not asking right, but finally she folds her front legs and goes down. He tries to say *hoosta* more like Bonnie, and Gertrude rises quicker than she knelt.

'Good job,' Sully says. It makes Alex glow inside. 'We'll make a camel driver out of you yet.'

When it's time to go, Alex retrieves Jago and takes him the long way round the house to the northern side of the yards. Jago is prancing and showing the whites of his eyes, but he's not trying to escape. 'I'll lead the way,' Alex says to Bonnie.

'Yep, yep,' she teases. 'I know this is for Jago's benefit.' She follows him on Ruby, leading the other two camels tail to nose, like those old explorer photos of camel strings.

Bonnie calls out from behind him, 'Where shall we go first?'

Alex turns his head. 'When?'

She flashes that massive smile. 'When Jago is used to Gertrude and Asmaan.'

Bonnie's optimism makes a light flare inside him. It's small, but he feels brighter than he's felt since Dad started to get sick.

'Why don't you take me to a place now? What's your favourite?' she calls.

He's about to say she's seen it when she cuts in, 'Besides Rocky Peak.' She's sharp. At this rate he'll have to be careful what he's thinking. 'It'll give the camels a bit of exercise.'

He turns Jago's head slightly to the north-east. 'Okay,' he calls.

They arrive at the dry creek. Alex dismounts and ties Jago to a branch. The horse backs up around the other side of the tree, putting the trunk between himself and the imagined threat. He stares at the camels, nodding his head up and down, and gives a snort.

Alex laughs. 'You are funny, Jago. When will you realise they don't care about you?'

Bonnie leaves the camels sitting and ties Ruby to a tree at the recommended distance from Jago. The other two camels start eating weeds in front of them, still tied to Ruby. 'They don't mind staying tethered?' Alex asks.

'Nup, they're used to it. They often go on treks strung together with rope like this.'

They walk down the bank and survey the creek.

'This place has memories,' he says.

Bonnie nods, respectful.

'Mum remembers swimming in it as a teen. My grandpa used to bring water from here into the troughs in this paddock.'

Bonnie looks across at him. 'What about you?'

'I can remember it running after a rain. Not real deep, but enough to get wet in. I was little though.'

'We've always had droughts, Pop says.'

'Yeah, seems worse now.'

She nods and sits on the bank. Alex crouches beside her, gazing at the orange-cracked sand of the creek bed. Bonnie stares at the tree trunks and broken branches filling the creek. 'Why are the fallen trees still here? If you had a flash flood you'd be in trouble.'

'Yeah. We haven't got around to moving them.' Dad's not up to doing jobs like this right now, but Alex doesn't say so. 'Maybe I could get the tractor down here and shift those in case it rains.'

'That's what I call hope, Alex.' Then she switches the subject.

'You know all the stuff we're doing at school about climate change? My uncle up near Marree married a Yura lady, and my cousins say we need to plant things that their ancestors used to plant, to help the environment cope with climate change. A lot of the European planting and animals have wrecked the ecosystem here. I don't mean to be rude about sheep; look at us with camels. But we could help by using plants that get the ground back into balance. Stop the erosion. It's not too late.'

His interest is piqued. 'That's like Josh talking about making more use of saltbush.' Anything to help stop the damage made by whirly-whirlies sounds good.

'Yep. And grasses native to the area. And cocksfoot as a hay crop even, when we can crop again.'

'Why's that?'

'It has a deep root system and is a good forage plant.'

Alex thinks about it. 'We could plant more native trees that don't need as much water. Melaleucas maybe.' It makes him think of his herb and veggie garden. 'When we get the camels settled, would you like to see my herb garden? Dad helped me plant it for Mum.'

'Sure, I'd love to.'

Jago is calmly grazing around the tree when they return. Bonnie pats his nose. 'You'll be used to me and the camels in no time.' It's the first time she's tried to touch him. He doesn't pull away as much as Alex thought he would.

'He may be getting used to camel smell after all,' he says.

Bonnie laughs. 'He's still twenty-five metres from them.' She mounts Ruby, says, 'Hoosta,' and the string of camels make their way to the paddock closest to the shed with Jago in the lead.

Alex shades his eyes to see ahead. A guy is waiting by the gate to the paddock. 'Oh no, it's Dad.'

Ten

His dad doesn't wait until they get close enough to hear him speak. Instead, he shouts, 'What do you think you're doing with those camels?'

Alex hopes he's talking to him and not Bonnie. They walk closer. 'The camels will head off any feral dogs, Dad.'

'Camels are bad news, son. They'll knock over the troughs, drink all the water out of the tank.'

Alex hesitates. He hadn't thought of the water they'd drink. 'It's still worth it, Dad.'

'They'll make more work than they're worth.'

Alex feels anger and embarrassment rise up. 'We don't want to lose more sheep, do we, Dad?' It's an underhand blow, and his dad falters.

'Here's Rachael and Tangi,' Bonnie says quietly.

'Go to Alex,' his mum says to Tangi, who races over and sits by Jago. 'Tom, there you are.' His mum sounds like a nurse with a medicine trolley. 'It's time for your dinner.' She waves to Alex and Bonnie to keep going as she leads Dad away.

Alex and Bonnie are quiet as they leave Jago at the shed to eat hay. It's a relief that Bonnie doesn't ask about Dad. How could he explain? 'Why don't you ride with me?' Bonnie says. She tells Ruby to sit, and Alex climbs on behind her.

'It feels amazing to be up this high,' he says, but the thrill of it can't take away the remorse at what he said to his dad.

They lead Asmaan and Gertrude to the sheep paddocks. 'Will they be okay one in each paddock?' Alex finally says. 'I guess they can talk over the fence. We don't put all the sheep in one paddock, not enough feed.' *When the rain finally comes*, he adds silently.

Bonnie raises her eyebrows. 'Guess so. Try it and see. Hoosta!' and Ruby kneels to let them off. Bonnie unties Gertrude, then mounts Ruby again to take Asmaan through the gate and into the next paddock.

The camels look around and don't seem fazed by the fence between them. They set to chewing up a thorny acacia on the fence line. Meanwhile, Lanky trots up to Alex and nudges him. 'What's she doing?' Bonnie asks.

'Saying hello. This is the one I bottle-fed. Now she thinks she's human. She's got long legs and good wool, and Dad was hoping to breed from her.' Alex shakes his head.

'What happened?'

'She won't let the ram get near her. She's such a snob – always away from the mob, feeding by herself. That's why I've been careful with this new one. Made sure a ewe would feed her and teach her how to be a sheep.' Alex picks up the orphan lamb. It's still smaller than the others and easy to spot.

'Can I hold it?'

'Here.'

The lamb's legs dangle down to Bonnie's knees. 'It's so docile.' Even though they're both shook up about the incident with Dad, Alex can see how pleased Bonnie is with the lamb.

'That's lambs for you. As soon as you pick them up they go quiet. Not like kelpie pups. Hey, Tangi! Weren't you a can of worms?' Tangi yips, then sniffs the lamb's legs to make sure it's okay.

After they ride back to the shed on Ruby, Alex shows Bonnie around the back of the house to see the garden. They sit quietly, Alex still chewing over what he said to his dad. He'll need to apologise. Bonnie glances at him, a question mark on her face, and he swivels his hat in his hands. Maybe he needs to tell her.

'This garden is all I have of Dad at the moment.' He bites his lip. It's not what he wants to say.

Bonnie doesn't jump in and ask what he means. Instead, she shakes Tangi's front paw, then frowns, turns the paw over. Tangi gives a slight whimper.

'Alex, she doesn't have any pads on her paw.' She lifts up the other front paw. 'All her paws like this? I thought she couldn't run far because she's old.'

Alex takes in a long breath. Everything to do with his dad is hard to talk about, and the more he doesn't tell the harder it gets, and now he doesn't even know where to start. But Bonnie helps. She waits for him to think it through, stares out over the paddock so there's no pressure. It gives him strength to finally speak.

'Dad isn't well.'

Bonnie nods as Alex licks his lips, deciding what to say next. He watches Tangi grinning at Bonnie. He can begin with Tangi.

'A fire came through here early last year. The ground was as dry as tinder. It missed most of our property except two paddocks – which both had sheep in them. Tangi was with the sheep in the northern paddock. We didn't tell her to go, but that's where she was when Dad went to look for her. He found her in the middle of the paddock, with the sheep rounded up on the only unburnt patch. She must have continually moved them out of the way of the fire. But her feet were burned – she couldn't walk.' He gulps. Can he say it? He takes in a wobbly breath. 'Dad . . . he carried her out of the burnt paddock to the quad bike and brought her home . . . carried her into the house. He was crying, saying *sorry, sorry*, to Tangi as if the fire was all his fault.'

Bonnie's silent, watching him, then says, 'She knew which way to move them?'

Alex nods. 'Even when the wind changed.'

Bonnie's 'Oh' is quiet and respectful. 'Tangi saved your sheep.'

'Only the ones in that paddock.' He has to finish it. 'Dad had to shoot the others that couldn't survive. He buried them near the dam. It's like it broke him.' Alex's voice cracks. He hadn't thought of that before, but it's true. His dad is broken inside; his eyes have never regained their sparkle. 'The rural volunteers came soon after, helping to fix the burnt fences, cutting the wire into pieces, but Dad never picked up. It was like shooting the sheep took his hope of buying more, took his hope for rain and better days.'

Bonnie puts a hand on his, and Alex doesn't say any more about sheep. 'Mum and I thought Tangi needed a new name. She was called Kangi – she used to jump a lot.' He tries to grin. 'She was such a cute puppy.'

'I'll bet.'

'We changed her name to Tangi. It rhymes, so she had no trouble with it.'

'Tangi, fire dog,' Bonnie whispers. 'That's a beautiful story.' She looks across at Alex, her eyes bright, and he nods.

'Tell me more about this garden,' Bonnie says, looking around, and Alex is grateful for the change of topic. 'There's more than herbs here.'

'Most of it died, but the succulents like the aloe vera are doing okay. We never had a lawn here, just ground cover. That's gone too. The geraniums are pretty unkillable, though.'

'Aloe vera is good for healing sunburn or smearing on scars.'

He nods. Maybe he needs some aloe vera.

'Some of those grasses my cousins were talking about would look good here,' Bonnie says.

'Yeah – stop the brown dirt showing through, eh?'

'You know what's the best thing about native plants?' She doesn't wait for Alex to answer. 'They capture carbon dioxide before it can enter the atmosphere to contribute to climate change.'

'I didn't hear that at school.'

Bonnie smiles. 'Native plants help our environment. I've heard if we only planted about five per cent of our farmland with these plants, it would really help meet our carbon targets.'

The breeze picks up and the windmill clangs as it spins.

'You still use a windmill? Not solar panels?'

Alex shrugs. 'Dad did the research. Discovered windmills are still more efficient – they produce more energy and use less energy. Less carbon dioxide, as well. They don't have to rely on sunshine, either. Guess that's why there's a wind turbine farm not far from here.'

Bonnie nods and looks at the layout of the herb and veggie garden. Some of it is planted in old cut-up iron tanks – the rest is made from wood.

'It's reticulated,' Alex says. 'You put the hose in the pipe of the wicking bed, and it waters the plants without the sun evaporating the moisture.'

'This is incredible. You cut up a tank?'

'Dad did that. We weren't using it.'

'Where did you get the railway sleepers?'

'Further north.'

'They're heavy.'

'Yeah, Dad helped me make this for Mum. I got the idea online.' Making the garden with Dad had felt so good. Maybe he should get him to help make another gift.

'Alex, this herb garden is like a micro-sustainable farm! Can I take a photo? My cousins would love to see it. Could they put it in their project?'

'Yeah.' Alex is reeling at the sustainable bit – that's what he wants to do with the whole farm when he's old enough. To have a biodiverse range of plants, with shelter belts for little birds and insects; use different seeds like peas and wheat for hay, even get the sheep eating grain instead of hay. 'Jago helped too. He pulled the sleepers off the truck up to here.'

Bonnie grins as she bends to hug Tangi. 'Did you help too, Tangi?' Tangi yips, liking the attention.

'Tangi helps with everything, don't you, girl?' She sits up and looks at Alex earnestly, like, *Why wouldn't I?* 'Kelpies are so suited for work on the land here – they were bred for it. After a hard day's work she wants to do it all over again.'

'Wonder why they're called kelpies?'

'A Scottish guy named them that after a folktale – the horses that lived in the sea were called kelpies.'

'Really?' Bonnie's eyes shine.

'Dad told me; he grew up with horses.' *Dad again.* Alex lets out a sigh. 'I wanted Mum to have this herb garden because she loves cooking. We used to cook together.'

'Do you cook by yourself?'

Alex hesitates. 'Just breakfast. Cooking's more fun with Mum.'

Bonnie faces him. 'Why don't we cook tea for your parents? Pop and I cook all the time. Do you have mince?'

Alex nods, wondering why her mum doesn't cook. 'In the freezer.'

Bonnie indicates the herbs. 'You've got basil, oregano, parsley. We can make bolognaise.'

Alex grins. 'You eat Italian?'

'Yeah, Mum loves Italian.' She smiles gently. 'Pop likes curries best, but we eat everything. Do you like Indian curries?'

'Sure. Ours mightn't be as good as your pop's, though.'

'Let's make an Afghan curry instead. I'll grab some of this spinach. It's great in curries. Pop calls it saag.' Bonnie pulls out her phone. 'I'll text Sully.'

'That'll work better under the ghost gum. It's on higher ground.'

She grins. 'Like our place. At least coverage is good on Rocky Peak, but that's a bit of a trek just to send a message.' She finishes the text. 'I bet kids in the city have fast internet. Do you ever wish you were there?'

Alex shakes his head as they get up to walk to the house. 'Never. We've visited Dad's parents in the suburbs, but all fences you can't see through and the constant noise of the traffic made me claustrophobic. I'd rather hear magpies, willie wagtails and sheep. The white owl hooting at night. Even a flock of screeching cock-atoos or galahs. Though the beach was a bit like here.'

'How?'

'The horizon is just as far away. The sea heaving – all that space – just like our paddocks. Just a different colour.'

'You wouldn't be able to have Jago in the city, either.'

'Nor Tangi. She'd feel caged. She's quieter now she's older, but she still likes to run a lot and jump fences. In February at shearing time, she was running on the backs of the sheep, guiding them through the gates into the shearing shed and out again.' He grins. Even his mum shore a few sheep that day. His mum is surprising.

Bonnie's mouth is a perfect *O*. 'Tangi jumps fences?'

'More than fences. She used to win awards for jumping when she was younger.' They reach the veranda.

'You happy for me to come inside?'

Alex is amazed all over again at how it's like Bonnie knows what he's feeling, like, *What if Dad doesn't want her there.*

'Yeah, it'll be fine.' Maybe his dad will be asleep. Or will have forgotten what he was upset about. Alex hopes so – he doesn't want to miss out on cooking with Bonnie. At the door he sweeps his arm in a mock welcome, and she laughs.

Inside, Alex takes lamb from the freezer and puts it in hot water to thaw.

Bonnie chops onions while he finds the garlic, ginger and chillies.

'Coriander?' she asks.

'Too hard to grow here.' He hands her ground coriander.

'This will do.'

By the time Alex's mum walks in from work the curry is simmering and the rice almost cooked. 'What's this?' she says.

Bonnie looks up. 'I hope you don't mind, Rachael, but I stayed to help Alex cook tea for you all.'

Mum smiles. 'I don't mind at all – thank you. I'll have a shower.'

Bonnie looks at Alex as his mum retreats to the bathroom. 'Is she happy about it?'

Alex nods, thinking of his mum's smile. 'She never gets the chance to shower and change before tea.'

The curry is a success. So is Bonnie. His dad doesn't say much, and never mentions camels. Alex can't believe how Bonnie draws his mum into talking. When it's just the three of them around the table at night they run out of things to say, but Bonnie talks about their life up north near Farina. Mostly about her dad and Pop. Not much about her mum, Alex notices.

After fruit and ice-cream, Dad says to Bonnie, 'You're a good friend to Alex. Don't let those camels cause any damage now.'

They all stare at him.

'Dad?' Alex pauses. 'I'm sorry I shouted at you and said what I did.'

Dad nods. 'Your mother explained that you're protecting the sheep.' Then he stands. 'I'm off to bed.'

Alex checks his mum's face. Her eyes are shining with unshed tears.

Before much longer, Bonnie says goodbye and runs out to text Sully to come get her.

Alex picks up a torch and takes Bonnie to the shed where they left Ruby. Jago is quiet, just snuffling a bit.

'He's getting used to her,' Bonnie says.

'Yeah. Thanks for cooking with me.'

'Sweet,' she says.

Sully's ute comes up the track to the shed and turns around.

'See ya.' Bonnie hops in the ute.

'You bet.'

'G'day, Alex.' Sully ties Ruby's nose rope to the tow bar. Then they drive very slowly down to the main road. Alex grins. *Guess they've done that before.*

He walks back inside to help his mum with the dishes, but they're in the dishwasher. She's enjoying a coffee in the lounge room. 'Bonnie's a nice girl,' she says.

'I showed her the herb garden. That's what started her wanting to cook.'

'That herb garden made me want to cook too.' She sounds wistful. Alex doesn't want to spoil the moment, so he tries to keep quiet. But he can't help himself. 'You could cook with me.'

Her smile is a shadow of her usual one. 'Let's do more of it from now on.' She finishes her cup, sets it down on the side table and gazes at him. It's the most focused she's been on him all these months. 'Alexander, I'm sorry – I know I've been distant . . .' She stops, then tries again. 'It's been difficult lately.'

Alex nods. She's not wrong there.

Eleven

‖‖

Early on Sunday Alex wakes to find the wind is up – and so is Dad.

'There's a weather alert for dust storms,' he says as soon as Alex walks into the kitchen. Alex's dad checks the Bureau of Meteorology app constantly, so he would have been expecting this since last night. It's strange but good to see him up so early, just like the old days, even if he is fuelled by anxiety.

He and Alex go outside, where they find the windmill already cranking. Dad pulls the chain to close the tail so the blades won't be damaged. 'It's weather like this that brought the fire,' he says to Alex. 'Better look at the sheep.'

Alex isn't worried – the danger alert is for further north. 'I'll see to them – it's just a dust storm, Dad.'

After feeding the animals and collecting eggs, Alex takes Jago for a ride to check on the food and water for the sheep. And to make sure the camels are behaving themselves. Tangi pads behind them.

The smallest lamb is under a tree with its surrogate mother. He gives it a cuddle. 'I see you're thriving.' The lamb relaxes in his arms. Tangi wants to sniff the lamb too. 'You do a good job, girl,' Alex tells her.

Gertrude and Asmaan are further away, close together on either side of the fence. Alex ties Jago to the tree and walks over there, feeling the wind growing stronger – he has to hold his hat when it gusts. The sky is still clear above, though.

Asmaan and Gertrude hang around him like Tangi does, and he wonders if they'll be capable of fighting off a wild dog. They don't mind Tangi. Alex smells a bit like camel himself after patting them, but Jago doesn't act up much on the way home. 'You're getting used to the smell.' Jago shakes his head and snorts, like, *You've got to be kidding, mate.*

It's when Alex lets Jago in the home paddock that he notices the light is fading. The sky to the north is a peachy colour, but on the horizon there's a huge orange wave. It's rolling in quick. 'Looks like the dust storm is closer than they thought, Tangi.' She barks. 'Yeah, I know, I'll get Jago back.' He whistles and the horse appears at the fence, the whites of his eyes showing. After camels, dust storms are Jago's least favourite thing. 'C'mon, boy. It's the shed for you this morning. It should be over soon.' Jago is likely to run into the barbed wire fence during the storm. He could do a lot of damage to himself.

His mum will be shutting all the windows, rolling up towels for under the doors. Alex hopes Dad will be helping. The wind is rising, that orange wave surging closer like a tsunami. There'll be a whole pile of red dirt from up north dumped on their property today.

Then he thinks of the camels. How would he face Bonnie and Sully if he didn't check Gertrude and Asmaan were okay and something happened to them when the dust arrived? Alex races over to the ute to drive to their paddocks. Tangi leaps on the tray.

Dust is blowing over the paddocks already. He thought he had more time. Tangi jumps down before he gets out to inspect the sheep again, but they're huddled up together for safety. He can't see the orphan lamb – it must still be with its stepmum. Lanky is on the edge of the mob and baas to him. He and his mum will have to check them for pink eye tomorrow.

A gust nearly knocks him over – he can see less than a step in front of him now. He hears a groan close by. Gertrude. She's sitting, her back to the storm. He stumbles over to pat her and she grunts. 'You seem okay, Gertrude. I guess Asmaan is too.' Her eyes look weird, like they've turned white, but she seems happy.

He has to crawl, but he manages to get back to the ute. He nearly loses the door when he gets it open – it bangs back against the front-wheel mudguard. 'Up, Tangi!' She jumps through to the passenger side, and he struggles with both hands to pull it around and slam it shut while dust blasts into the cabin.

He drives a short way, but can't find the gate. The windscreen wipers are no help. He can't keep driving – he may run over a sheep. Lanky could be hanging around.

Alex coughs – maybe it wasn't clever to come, but at least he feels reassured about the camels. He can imagine the orange-red tsunami crashing across them. The ute pitches and rocks. This seems stronger than their usual dust storm – surely the drought's fault again.

Tangi whimpers and licks his hand. Alex can hardly see her with dust swirling in the cabin. 'It's okay, girl. Good thing we got Jago in. Wish we had masks, Tangi.' But the masks his dad used for spraying hay crops are all in the shed. Dust is still seeping inside the ute, even though he makes sure the windows are up. It's pouring in now through the vents. He won't be able to hold his breath for an hour, which is how long a dust storm can last for. 'It will be over soon,' he says to Tangi, mostly to calm himself. 'Get down on the floor.' She obeys and stops whimpering. 'We just have to keep calm and wait it out.'

Alex lies across the front seat, curling round the gearstick to keep his face clear of dirt. He hopes his mum knows he'll be okay. That reminds him – he sits up to try the UHF. It's always kept on the same channel.

'Mum, I'm okay, over.' Nothing. He tries again, and this time there's a crackle. He can hardly hear her. 'I'm in the ute. Tangi's with me, over.' He can't distinguish what she's saying, but at least she'll know he's fine.

He pats Tangi but she's gone quiet. He touches her side and feels it moving. He decides to follow her example.

It seems like forever, but finally the noise of the wind subsides and visibility improves. Phew, that's over. He's never been out for the duration of a dust storm before.

Alex turns the key. The engine splutters and stops. He tries again, careful not to flood the engine. He waits before trying a third time – it comes to life. Phew again.

'Okay, Tangi. Let's go home.'

Visibility is poor, like looking through orange-brown glass, but he finds the gate, gets out to open it. He doesn't get blown away like before. It's definitely easing. He puts the ute away and lets Tangi inside. The kitchen floor has centimetres of dirt over it, and dirt is dribbling down the walls. Definitely one of their worst storms.

His mum rushes over and hugs him. He thought he'd get told off first.

'Alexander! I'm glad you're safe.'

'Were you worried?' His face must look like he's been paintballing.

'No.' Then she smiles. 'Just a bit.'

'Is Dad okay?'

Her face falls. 'Unfortunately, the high wind reminded him of the fire. So we can add dust storm to his list of triggers: fire, sheep, guns and now extreme wind.'

'The wind that stirred up the fire was travelling over eighty kay an hour. This wasn't that fast, was it?'

She shakes her head. 'Try explaining that to your dad.'

The dust storm passes over before the hour is up, but they spend the next two hours sweeping and mopping. Alex uses the broom on the walls and pulls all the dust to the floor so they can vacuum it up. On the floor it looks like red sand. 'I reckon half the desert from the north just got dumped on us.' His mum smiles at him and he grins.

The sky is still murky, but Alex goes out to the ghost gum to text Bonnie to see how they fared.

You all okay?

He waits while it sends. Takes ages. He hopes she can receive it, and adds another one.

I checked on the camels. All okay.

Then she answers.

They can close their nostrils.

No kidding?

Two sets of eyelashes and three sets of eyelids. One set of eyelids closes over the eye and it's transparent so they can still see.

So that's why Gertrude's eye looked weird. Can I come over later?

Pop says our door is always open to you.

Roger from the neighbouring property turns up to see if they need help. Dad won't come out of his room, so Roger and Alex clean out the troughs together. 'I think the dust storm has upset Dad,' Alex says.

'The wind even reminded me of the fire. The wind that day was like a giant blowtorch. At least today it was only dust.'

'Hope we don't lose too much water from the troughs.'

'She'll be right, mate.'

Before tea, Alex rides over to Bonnie's place on Jago. He thinks of it as the Camel Farm now, like people in town. He ties Jago to a tree near the camel yards, but shortens the rope as usual. He hopes Jago can't tell he's getting closer to the camels.

This time Pop and Sully are building what looks like a high aviary around two trees. The poles are up and the men are stretching wire netting, like chicken wire, but stronger, around the sides. A wooden platform is attached in one corner.

Pop sees him first. 'Hoy, we need your help, young man.'

'Sure. What can I do?' It makes Alex feel wanted.

Pop climbs down from the ladder. Alex still marvels at what the old bloke can do, being ninety-five. 'We have to get netting over the top and I can't reach that far. The storm set us back – we hadn't finished nailing the netting down before it hit.'

Alex grins. This is the first time he's heard Pop admitting his limitations. 'I can help.'

'Just wait until Sully's finished with nailing in the walls.'

Bonnie comes out of the house. 'Hey, Alex. I've got something to show you.'

Pop calls out. 'Don't spook it.'

'Aw, would we do that, Pop?'

His eyes crinkle at her as he shakes his head.

Alex wonders if Pop is referring to the joey. 'Is the joey sick?'

'Nup, I'll show you.' She takes Alex to the south side of the house. 'Here she is.'

The roo is eating grass in a small enclosure. Alex leans over and strokes her. She's too big now to hold – what if she jumped down his shirt and scratched him with her claws?

'She's getting used to us. Pop's a sook when it comes to baby animals. C'mon, Alex.'

He can tell Bonnie's got more news – it's racing over her face.

She leads him to the house, but they don't go inside. She takes him to the closest window. It looks like a spare room with boxes and a desk.

'Look in the corner closest to you.'

Alex strains his neck to look in, then sucks in a breath. 'Really? You've got an eagle in your house? What did your mum say?'

Bonnie doesn't answer about her mum. 'It got hit by a ute and its wing is broken.'

Alex stares at the crumpled mass of tan and gold feathers lying on the rug, and his eyes tear up. They're supposed to be majestic, soaring in the sky, not scrunched in a corner of a room. Bonnie puts a hand on his back. 'Don't feel bad. I cried too when I first saw her.'

Alex blinks back the tears and swallows. 'The aviary is for her?'

Bonnie nods. 'Once their wings break they usually can't fly high again, because the bones can crack under the strain.'

Alex stares at her, wondering how she knows that.

She raises her chin. 'Pop told me. He loves birds – has a way with them. You can't tell an eagle not to fly high, can you?'

Alex shakes his head. 'Nah. You can't. Was she on the road?'

'Yep. There's no food left for them in the bush, so they're eating roadkill.'

'And they can't fly up quickly – they need a wind current to rise high in the air, and there isn't time for them to gain any height when a vehicle is approaching, even at regular speed.' Alex knows that much at least. His grandad has told him to watch for eagles when he starts driving on the road.

'Yep.' She stares at the eagle. 'It's fully grown but young, not many dark feathers.'

Just then, Pop gives a hoy. 'We're ready for you, son.' It makes Alex grin at Bonnie.

'Pop actually admitted he couldn't spread the netting on the roof.'

Bonnie's eyes widen. 'You're kidding?'

Alex warms with the realisation that Bonnie livens him up like Lily used to. Imagine having Lily back in the house, cheering up his dad and himself at breakfast, to cook with in the evening.

Alex climbs up the ladder – it looks like a construction site ladder, with three extensions. No wonder Pop doesn't like to climb it. It even makes Alex nervous, but he's determined to push through it. Hasn't he climbed the windmill plenty of times when his mum wasn't around?

He climbs up so quickly, it's almost reckless. When he reaches the top, Sully throws the netting across to him.

'Just stretch it over to the hooks on the side,' Sully says. 'I'll secure it all afterwards.'

It doesn't take long, and when Sully gives the nod, Alex climbs down the ladder to join Pop. He's talking to Jago and the horse is eating from his hand. As Alex arrives, Pop says, 'You don't mind me giving him a treat?' Alex shakes his head. 'He's a fine gelding. How old?'

'Three years.'

'I reckon he'll be used to the camels in no time at all.'

Alex grins. 'Yeah. He doesn't realise how close he's getting.' He chews his lip. Now would be a good time to ask Pop a private question.

'Pop, I've never seen Bonnie's mum – is she sick? Would it help if my mum came to visit her?'

Pop keeps patting Jago. 'What has Bonnie said?'

'Nothing much. Just mentions when her mum likes stuff she does or that she doesn't mind having Jago over or me. Is she . . . is she bedridden?' Alex hopes he doesn't sound nosy.

'No.' Pop puts a hand on Alex's shoulder.

'Just before when I asked what her mum said about an eagle in the house, she didn't answer, and I don't want to . . . you know . . .'

Pop nods slowly.

'And she often says what her mum helps her with, but she's never introduced me. I mean, does her mum not like visitors?' Alex finds that hard to understand when Bonnie is so friendly, and Sully and Pop too.

Pop faces Alex square on. 'Son, her mum died when Bonnie was a little tacker.'

Alex frowns at him. 'Died?'

Pop nods. 'Car accident.'

'But Bonnie . . . she . . .' Alex doesn't know what to say.

'She'll tell you when she's ready.'

The feeling that rises inside takes Alex by surprise. It hurts, and his breath comes fast. How could Bonnie do that? Let him think her mum has been alive all this time?

Twelve

||||||||||||||||||||||||||||||||||||||||||||||||||||||||||||||||||||||||||||||||||||||||

On the bus in the morning, Alex concentrates on other things – he doesn't want to think badly of Bonnie. If he does, he might say something to ruin their friendship. Fortunately, Harry takes up all his attention. 'So how did the dust storm affect your place, mate?'

'Lost some water from the troughs, but Roger helped me clean them out. A few sheep have pink eye. What about the cattle on the station?'

Harry grins. 'They're pretty indestructible. Used to anything. Just sat and faced the other way. That's what they did when we had that fire – sat and didn't move even though the fire passed just a couple of hundred metres from them. Kept the calves in the middle.'

'Impressive.' It reminds Alex of Tangi protecting the sheep.

At school, Bonnie is telling the little kids about the habits of eagles and how her Pop will heal their rescue one. Everyone wants to see it. Alex grins. Sully and Pop wouldn't mind lots of visitors, which makes him think of

Bonnie's mum again. Does Bonnie just want to keep her alive in her mind?

Summer screws up her nose before class when she hears about the eagle. 'You shouldn't mess with nature. You can't keep an eagle in an aviary.'

Bonnie's face is immovable. 'It won't be there forever. Pop has a way with birds.'

'Huh. If you put an eagle in a cage it'll be trapped there forever—' All of a sudden, Summer's face crumples and she rushes from the room. Alex and Bonnie stare after her.

'What's up with her now?' Harry says. No one answers him.

Saturday rolls around again. After a full-on week, Alex is ready to lie in bed awhile. He thinks again about Bonnie and her mum. He knew she was a safe person to tell about his dad's illness. Doesn't she think he, Alex, is a safe person? Maybe she will if he acts normal and doesn't push her to tell him.

Alex hopes Dad will be more positive today. It's an effort to keep on top of things when he isn't. Maybe he could ask Dad to help him water the herb garden and veggies. Constructing that garden together is a bright memory for Alex, and he hopes it's the same for Dad.

Dad's actually up in time for breakfast since it's later on Saturday. After bacon and eggs, Alex grabs the ram by the horns and asks Dad to come outside to help with the chooks. Once the eggs are collected, washed and put in the cooler, Alex says, 'Let's check the herb garden.'

His dad doesn't answer but he follows Alex around the back.

'The aloe vera is doing okay still,' Alex comments for something to say.

'Hmm.' His father gets the hose and starts watering. Alex smiles at him. 'What do you suggest I plant now to make the area more like a garden?' *Since we lost the front one*, he thinks.

'Some more succulents?'

'Like those ones with the orange flowers in the War Memorial Park in town?'

His father nods, watching the water making little wells, then he pops the hose in the tube to water underneath. They don't say much more, but Alex can feel a connection that they haven't had for a long time. They stand in companionable silence until his father turns off the tap. 'Don't forget to check the tanks in a week or two,' he says.

Alex grins. It's almost like old times.

His next job is seeing to the sheep. He's been out there a few evenings on Jago or the quad bike, just checking that the camels haven't killed the sheep like some people expect. So far so good.

He drives the ute to take two bales of hay for the sheep, whistling for Tangi to jump onto the tray. He can see her in the rear-vision mirror, grinning over the edge. It's great pretending he's a farmer already. His mum's grandfather was doing a farmer's work before he was thirteen. Had to get up at three in the morning to bring the horses in from the paddock and feed them because then they had to wait over an hour after eating before they could work. He could even run a plough with seven Clydesdales. Alex would love to have seen that. There are photos – old sepias. He could show Bonnie; she'd be interested.

His breath catches in his throat at the thought of Bonnie – and her mum. Why does that bother him so much? He feels like he doesn't know Bonnie anymore.

Alex slows the ute. The sheep seem quiet, relaxed, all gathered in one corner of the paddock where the biggest gum is. Good shade. It's hard to spot the orphaned lamb now – she has grown and blends in with the others, and is starting to eat by herself. Gertrude is standing nearby chewing her cud, like a soldier on guard duty.

The sheep in the next paddock are not far away, grazing. Where's Asmaan? Tangi gives a bark and jumps down, sniffs the sheep to make sure they are okay. She drops to let them know she doesn't want them to move. It's like she's counting them. Then she jumps the fence and races across the next paddock. Alex follows out through the gate and spots the male camel as he drives up the rise. Tangi gives a few barks, sniffs a heap on the ground, then sits on her haunches beside it until Alex gets out of the ute.

'What have you found, Tangi?' Asmaan groans and doesn't look put out that Tangi thinks she's done the finding.

Not far from Asmaan's front hooves is a carcass. Alex squats beside it; probably been dead a few hours, its head squashed. It's big like a bull-mastiff – a similar size to the dog he saw on Rocky Peak.

Alex stands up. 'So, Asmaan, you kicked a feral dog's head in. If only the kids at school could see this.' He pulls out his phone and takes a photo.

Asmaan groans again and snuffles Alex's head.

'Yeah, you're a clever boy. You've saved us a sheep this morning, maybe more.'

How many times have the camels just run the dog off? It must have become desperate to come close enough for Asmaan to kick it. Tara's words about camels being ferocious unwillingly come to mind, and Alex calls Tangi to his side. She pads over, passing under Asmaan's neck, but he doesn't react. Alex lets out a breath. It's a relief Asmaan doesn't see Tangi as a threat. He pats Asmaan's neck. 'Good work.'

He brings the ute closer. The dog is much heavier than a dingo, even though it's seen better days. He manages to drag it to the ute and pulls it up onto the tray, then ties a rope around it. He stands on the ute roof rack to check there are no more dead sheep. Though if there were, Tangi would tell him.

'Up,' he says to Tangi and she jumps onto the tray, keeping watch over the macabre load. Better show his mum, then he'll have to bury it with the tractor. His dad won't be able to help with this.

His mum gasps when she sees it. 'That's a monster, as big as the one that came around the chook shed. We'll have to bury it in the rubbish tip.'

Then she's on her phone to Sully, thanking him for his camels. Alex can hear her voice lifting and he grins. 'They caught the feral dog. No, no more dead sheep. Alexander checked. Yes, thank you, we'll keep them longer in case there's another dog. I don't know how to thank you.'

Alex drives the tractor out of the machinery shed, scoops up the dog and drives slowly to the rubbish dump in the easternmost paddock. He lowers the shovel over the hole so the dog falls in, then drives to the dam to dig a scoop of dirt. It takes a few scoops to cover the dog sufficiently so that nothing can dig it up.

By the time he's finished outside and had a shower, his mum has tea ready. It's his favourite: lasagne. 'Where's Dad?'

'He's eating tea watching footy. He seems content.'

Alex grins. 'Port Adelaide not playing, then?'

She smiles too. After Alex finishes, she puts her fork down. She doesn't say anything at first, just covers his hand with hers. 'Thanks for dealing with the dog, Alexander.'

He nods at her. It's for the best they didn't tell his dad about it. It might have set him back like handling the gun did weeks ago. It brought up the memories for Alex too, of his dad burying the burnt sheep after the fire.

Other farmers had to do that, too. Everyone in the district must still be worried about the drought conditions reducing their numbers of stock. He takes in a breath and says, 'It must have been hard for Dad, wasn't it? Shooting those sheep?'

Her eyes shut tight, and he can tell that everything else about her is shutting tight too. Then her hand curls around his. 'Yes, Alexander, it was. Too hard.'

She pulls in a quick breath. 'We need a little break. What say I take you and Bonnie into town tomorrow? I need to pick up meds for Tom, and the General Store's always open on Sunday.'

Alex grins. 'Thanks, Mum.' He runs out to text Bonnie.

In the morning they pick up Bonnie. 'Hello, Tangi,' she says first. 'Do you like going to town?'

Tangi yips. 'She likes the dog park,' Alex says. Tangi barks this time, like she knows what he said.

'She understands a lot of words,' Bonnie says. 'I've only been in town for school,' she adds. 'Sully hasn't had time to take me to look around.'

On the way in they drop their recycling in the bin at the town tip.

'Can you pick up bread and milk, please, Alex. And the mail.' Rachael lets Alex, Bonnie and Tangi off at the General Store while she goes to the pharmacy.

'Ta daaa,' Alex says in a pretend tour guide voice after he ties Tangi to a post. 'This is the General Store: grocery store, cafe and takeaway, gifts and Post Office all under one roof.'

Bonnie smiles. She likes the crafts. 'Look at these earrings made from drink-can pulls – they look like platinum. Anything can be upcycled.'

Just then Summer and Tara walk inside the store. Summer sees Bonnie and leans closer to Tara to whisper something. They're meant to hear Tara's reply. 'Yeah, she stinks so bad I thought she never gets away from those camels.'

'You're not wrong,' Summer says, staring straight at Bonnie. 'She'll have a camel face soon, whiskers coming out of her nostrils and ears.'

Bonnie ignores them and Alex admires the way she doesn't let it spoil her morning. The bread his mum likes isn't available, so they choose another brand.

'Shops in town can't always stock what they used to,' Alex says. 'Mum says people move away because they can't make a living – that's fewer people buying stuff. Fewer people going to the medical centre, so a doctor leaves. Other services close. It's even affected tourism. People want to come to a nice green place that makes them feel good, not where there are whirly-whirlies, the kangaroos are skinny and the paint is peeling off shop-fronts and houses because they don't have the money to do them up.'

Alex buys a picnic lunch of chicken and salad wraps and asks for the mail. There are a few letters and the *Stock Journal*, which he puts in the bag with the bread. He catches the return address on one of the letters: *Elders*. That's the agent who sends up a carrier to get their bales of wool and take them to Port Adelaide to sell. Money will be coming into their bank account in a week or two. He hopes it will be enough.

He leads Bonnie and Tangi down the street. 'There's

something special I want to show you. Tourists used to come interstate to see this before the pandemic.' They walk into an art gallery. 'This guy paints panoramic scenes. Imagine being this talented.' Bonnie climbs steps to see a painting stretching 360 degrees; it has to be two metres high. 'This is what it would look like if you'd just climbed St Mary Peak in the Flinders Ranges.'

'Incredible,' Bonnie whispers as she turns on the wooden platform in the huge circular shed.

They meet up with his mum at the War Memorial Park. 'We'll have lunch here,' Alex says, 'and Tangi can play in the dog park. The gardens aren't what they used to be, but these drought-resistant grasses and succulents are doing okay.'

Tangi barks as she jumps over tyres and crawls through a pipe tunnel, all set up like a children's playground. Bonnie laughs, and Alex wishes he could bottle the sound. Not much laughing in their house right now.

That night Alex sketches in his art journal. What sort of gift should he make for his mum's birthday? Maybe a sculpture for the garden, since nothing much grows at the moment. Thanks to his dad he can weld, and there's plenty of old farm junk lying around behind the sheds to make stuff with. His dad used to say if he had time he'd like to do that.

Once, Alex saw this photo of a horse an artist had made out of scrap metal. The horse was so lifelike it looked like it would shake its head. Alex wouldn't be able to create that, but as he's learning from Ms Penna, the art teacher, there's lots of different ways to do art. Mum's birthday is near the end of term; he'd better get a move on.

Thirteen

At school the next day, Summer brushes past Bonnie on the way into the classroom. 'Out of the way, camel girl.'

Alex bristles, but he gets a warning look from Bonnie to say nothing. Guess she wants to fight her own battles. Some of the older girls are in a huddle, glancing at him and Bonnie. Tara gives Bonnie one of her stiff stares. Alex tries to shrug off the dread. His annoyance about the way Bonnie talks of her mum fades as he hopes she's feeling okay. He frowns at Tara.

Tara bails up Bonnie at recess. There was a doco on TV last night about feral camels venturing further south than usual. Due to the drought, of course. They couldn't find water. Things are pretty bad if a camel can't find water.

Tara starts off. 'Feral camels are doing a lot of damage on the stations further north.'

Alex can tell where this is headed, but Bonnie doesn't miss a beat. 'Good thing my dad can save some of them then, hey. Less trouble.'

Summer snorts. 'They'll cause trouble here. They'll eat your place clean and then what will they do? And what about water? They drink a tankful in one go and your bore's dried up.'

Alex wonders how Summer, being a townie, could know so much about Gibsons' old place. He moves closer. But Bonnie tries a different approach. 'Our camels aren't feral. They're good for treks in the Flinders, which will help tourism here. They guard sheep. They can even be milked. We're building dairy yards – we've bought milking machines.'

Tara scoffs. 'They'll be roaming the district soon and my dad said if he finds one on our place he'll shoot it just like they should have in the desert.' It's like she didn't hear a word Bonnie said.

Summer says, 'The pub's always wanting more camel steaks for tourists.'

This is news to Alex, and he decides to intervene.

'You need to see Bonnie's place. It's well set up for camels. The fences could keep an eagle in.' Well, one eagle at least. He knows he's exaggerating, and Summer gives her a superior sniff.

'So *you* love camels now?' She looks from Alex to Bonnie and back to him. His heart sinks. He doesn't want his friendship with Bonnie pulled out into the open air, made into something it's not.

Summer's eyes narrow. Alex knows that look. Seems like she'll keep quiet for now if he toes her line. Trouble is, he doesn't know where Summer's line is. He can be in her bad books without even knowing what he's done.

The recess bell rings and they trail into the coolness of their classroom. At lunch Alex sits with Bonnie. She's a bit subdued. Not like herself at all. He thinks of a way to cheer her up. 'Would you like to help me do a job next Sunday? I have to check the water levels in the tanks.'

'Sure.'

'Let's see if Jago can handle being ten metres from Ruby.'

Her eyes light up. 'You're on. I bet he can't.'

'I bet he can.'

Harry has his say on the bus after Bonnie gets off. 'My old man's not keen on camels either. He reckons they shouldn't have been left to go feral. And how can camels that have been wild in the desert for a hundred years be capable of changing? You know what they've done. Ruined sheds, tanks, eaten cattle food. A mob of renegade camels can make a hell of a mess.'

Alex shrugs. 'You need to see Bonnie's camels. I'll show you one day when you're free.'

Harry grins. 'Good idea, but don't tell me you've fallen for camels and you have them on your place now?'

Alex sighs. 'They're protecting our sheep from wild dogs. They even killed one. We haven't lost a sheep since they came.' He pulls out his phone and shows Harry the photo he took. 'Look.'

Harry glances at it, then stares at him. 'You for real, mate?'

116

Alex nods. 'Mum agreed.'

Harry starts to speak and stops.

'It works with alpacas.'

'Alpacas, mate, are sooky pets. They'd sit on your lap if they could.'

Alex declines to say camels could be like that too. 'Take me up on my offer.'

'I might have to, you galah, to keep an eye on you. But I have to help my old man after school if there's no footy practice. That was the deal. I can come to school as long as I help with the cattle. He says he was a trainee jackaroo at my age.'

Alex stands up, ready for his stop. 'Come when there's no musters, then.'

'Sounds like a plan. About that photo . . .'

Alex raises his eyebrows.

'Don't show it around, people will think their dogs aren't safe next.'

They press their fists together as the bus stops. Alex steps down and gives a wave as the bus drives north. He doesn't know what he'd do without Harry. They've been mates since Harry first came in Year Two and they haven't had a difference of opinion before. He grins when he sees Tangi waiting for him and he ruffles her fur. 'Do you think you can go on a trek with me?' Tangi stares up at him. 'You'll need to ride with me on Jago. I hope you can still do that.'

Tangi yips twice. 'Was that "of course"?' Alex laughs. He's sure animals like Tangi understand more than most people think.

'C'mon, let's go home. Maybe Bonnie can give Ruby a wash, ha. Honestly, Jago is just going to have to bite the bullet, as Grandad would say.'

Alex has been looking forward to spending Sunday afternoon with Bonnie. He needs a break from worrying about his dad and now Summer getting upset. Like, what's up with her anyway? The ride up to Rocky Peak helps clear his head, and when Bonnie arrives she makes a fuss of Tangi, who barks once in welcome.

'Tangi, you've come too.' Bonnie looks up at Alex. 'How's that? She hasn't come this far before.'

'She's riding with me today. She used to when she was younger. I've left her home too much because of her paw-pads.'

'Clever girl.' Bonnie pats her and gives her a hug, getting her face washed in return.

She says hello to Jago. Ruby is still down the hill, but Jago isn't fussed.

'I'll take Jago down first if you want to follow? Don't want to make it too hard for him.'

'He's probably more used to them than you know because of Asmaan and Gertrude so close.'

'Up, Tangi.' She jumps; Alex catches her and settles her in front of him. He leads the way east to the first paddock they keep sheep in. Jago hardly acts up at all. Just snorts a few times. Much like Summer's snorts when she thinks she's right.

Dad and Roger checked the tanks a few weeks ago,

so Alex is expecting there to be at least a third of a tank of water left. He runs his hand down the tank. He frowns.

'What's wrong?' Bonnie asks.

'Only the bottom quarter feels cool. I'd better check to be sure.' He takes a torch out of his backpack, climbs up the old ladder attached to the tank and takes off the sieve. He puts his head in and shines the torch. 'Yeah, not much left.'

'You have to fill it?'

Alex comes back down the ladder. 'Yeah, we have a tank on the back of our truck that we cart water from the bore tank to the paddock tanks. Wish Mum would let me drive that. It means another job for her.'

'Could your dad do it?'

'Dad's not allowed to drive because of the meds he's on at the moment.'

She nods. 'I didn't mean to pry.'

Alex shrugs his shoulders. Guess it doesn't matter if Bonnie knows.

The next tank is lower. Even the water in the trough is low. 'I think the water is evaporating. We lost some during the dust storm, and then the cleaning out of the troughs. It can't just be the camels.'

'Camels don't drink the same amount in a paddock as when they're working,' Bonnie says.

'We'd better tell Mum.' They ride back to the shed where they leave Jago and Ruby, then walk up to the windmill. The tank there is on a higher stand with a tap and hose to pour into the outlet on the truck-tank. His mum hurries over. 'What is it, Alexander?'

'The tanks in the paddock are lower than usual and we need to fill them up today. I'll measure this one too.' He climbs the ladder attached to the tank stand, feels it with his hand. 'It isn't full,' he calls. 'We'd better tell Dad.'

Alex climbs down and his mum says, 'I'm not sure this is the sort of news Tom needs right now. The wool-sale notification was in the mail you picked up and he read it first. It wasn't good. This would be a huge worry on top of that.'

Alex tries not to think about what a smaller wool sale will do to the property. 'Do you think the water level's dropped in the bore?'

His mum runs a hand through her hair. 'If the water level's down, it may dry up like Gibsons' did. That's not far away.' She glances at Bonnie, who's moved away to look at the herb and veggie garden.

'We could still have different underground water than them, though.' He's learned about the underground Great Artesian Basin in school. Some of their underground water may even be coming from New Guinea.

'If it dries up it could be six months or six years before it comes back, if at all.' His mum sounds as low as his dad today.

'We ought to measure it.' Alex feels his frustration rise. The wool-sale figure must have really upset her.

She tightens her lips and thinks aloud. 'We'll have to cart mains water.' Alex has seen the standpipe for that a few kay from the town. 'We'd have to pay the district council – that's an expense we can't afford. Or we could sell the sheep. Won't get much for them—'

Alex cuts in. 'Let's cart what we have.'

It's like she can't hear him. 'The wool payment is the lowest we've ever had. We have so few sheep and lack of good feed. Less water affects the fleece. We'll have to live in town—'

'Mum!' She pulls her head up, and Alex lowers his voice a little. 'I'm sorry, but you sound like Dad. If the water is lower, we can still use what's left. We mustn't give up.' Isn't that what they've both told him all his life, teaching him resilience through every difficult time?

Just then his dad comes out of the house and walks up to them.

Bonnie meets him halfway. 'Hi, Tom, it's good to see you.' He smiles at her and Alex sighs in relief. Bonnie can always get a response from his dad.

When his dad reaches Alex and Mum, his tone is different. 'What's going on?'

Alex charges in. 'We need to measure the water level in the bore.'

His dad glances at the tank. 'You checked the bore tank?'

'Yeah, it's only two-thirds full.'

'It must be taking longer to come up.' Alex waits for him to make the connection. 'The water may be lower.'

Alex nods.

They measure the depth with a rope. Alex threads it down until he hears the *ping* of it touching water. His dad ties a string on the rope at ground level. 'Pull it up, son.' He has the measuring tape ready.

'How deep?' his mum asks. She and Bonnie crowd in to see.

'Thirty-three and a half metres.' He grunts. 'Lower than last time I checked.'

'What depth was that?' his mum asks.

'Thirty and a half metres.'

Alex whistles. Three metres lower. No wonder the tank's not full.

'We'll keep using it,' his dad says. 'If they have rain up in Queensland we may get the benefit of that.' It's the most positive thing Alex has heard his dad say in ages.

'Can I drive the truck?' Alex asks.

'No.' His mum's answer is swift. 'I will. You and Bonnie can guide the hose into the tank.'

After filling the truck-tank, Bonnie and Alex ride in the truck to siphon water into the tanks in the paddocks. Bonnie always seems to make a difference in whatever he is doing. Was his dad more positive at the windmill because Bonnie spoke to him first?

When they get back to the shed Jago is quiet, watching for them. He's not staring at Ruby. Alex goes up to Ruby to say hello and she plants a kiss on his head. Bonnie pulls out some crackers and juice from her back-pack. 'I think we deserve a picnic.'

Tangi sits beside them and Bonnie feeds her crackers. 'You are a very clever girl riding a horse.' Tangi grins with her tongue lolling out.

'Looks like we have a problem with water. It's all over when the bore dries up.'

Bonnie nods. 'Yep.' Then she brightens. 'But your dad was helping today – that's good, isn't it?'

He grins; just like Bonnie to see the bright side. 'I think I won the bet,' he says.

'Which one?'

'Jago is not rolling his eyes – yet look how close Ruby is.'

Bonnie chuckles. 'That's one bet I'm glad to lose.'

Fourteen

||||||||||||||||||||||||||||||||||||||||||||||||||||||||||||||||||||||||||||||||

Alex thought his dad would be feeling better this morning after helping with the water situation yesterday, but his dad won't get out of bed. There were times last year where his dad slept for days. Lately he's even been coming to the breakfast table – surely he won't slide back to staying in bed all day.

It's all too much. Alex doesn't even feel like taking breakfast to his dad. He grabs his backpack and marches out of the house. His mum calls after him. 'Alexander, we need to talk.' He pretends he doesn't hear while Tangi yips and runs in front of him.

'Go home,' he shouts. She turns, her tail between her legs. Alex feels bad, but he doesn't stop. 'I'll see you this arvo.' If Lily were here she would be helping with Dad and the feed run. And yesterday showed him how precarious their life on the property is. What if they had to live in town or sell because the bore dried up?

'Hey, Alex,' Bonnie says as soon as he sits beside her on the bus. He can't answer. So far today he's been mean to his mum and even to Tangi. He had better keep his mouth shut.

Bonnie is quiet for a while. He's certain she's looking at him but he won't look up. Then she leans forward on the seat. 'I've been thinking.'

It's her happy 'ideas' voice, and Alex can't help himself – he looks up. She's smiling at him as though he hasn't just ignored her. Bonnie's smile and enthusiasm do perk up his day, especially in the morning after a difficult breakfast with Dad or being awake half the night worrying about the bore.

'Those crafts at the General Store reminded me about upcycling. And remember that video about the carbon footprint of a plastic water bottle?' Alex nods. He hasn't forgotten it either. 'We could make things out of disused items, so they don't end up as landfill. Stuff can be reused so rubbish gets reduced. Landfills contribute to climate change because they release biogas, carbon dioxide as well as methane.' She grins at him. 'I've done some research. If landfills can be reduced by people recycling their rubbish, it will help our environment.'

Alex joins in. 'So landfills are ruining our atmosphere, and by reusing plastic we won't have to make new plastic. That way we can help save our atmosphere and also the environment.'

'Yep.' Bonnie pulls out a notebook. 'Each year we extract and use over ninety billion tonnes of raw materials like cellulose, coal, natural gas, salt and crude oil to make plastics. We only recycle nine per cent. Most plastics still end up as landfill.' She turns to Alex, her face shining. 'We can help cut the carbon footprint of plastic. Every time plastic is recycled the carbon footprint is less.'

'What sort of things?' Alex thinks of the sculpture he's creating in the shed when the jobs are done. It doesn't look much yet, so he's keeping it under wraps.

'Like recycling plastic bottles into seedling and plant pots – I saw that online. Did you know it takes over five litres of water to make one single-use water bottle?'

'That's way too much.' Alex thinks of their bore possibly drying up and the millions of plastic bottles that are made. This is messing with his head.

'Yep.'

Alex pulls his thoughts together. 'We have a lot of stuff lying around the back of our sheds.' That's what he's using for the sculpture.

When Harry jumps up the steps, Bonnie is still talking about it.

'You could start a club at school, Bonnie,' Harry says.

Alex isn't sure Harry is being serious; Bonnie obviously thinks he is. Her eyes grow huge. 'An upcycling club! Everyone could bring plastic stuff and we can turn it into useable things. There's a sewing machine at school. Maybe we could make bags or purses.'

'We could melt down plastic and make other things from it.' This is Harry.

Alex hates to put a spoke in the wheel, but he has to bring Bonnie and Harry down to earth. 'We'll have to find out how first. Like, what sort of a machine does it take to crush plastic or melt it? And besides, a club sounds more like something the little kids would be into.'

Bonnie's face falls slightly, and Alex is so sorry he hastens to lift it. 'We could ask Mr Clarke about it.' He says it just to bring the excited look back into her eyes.

'Yeah,' Harry chips in, 'and we could ask Kris to help with stuff too, on a day he's there, like Wednesday or Friday. He'd be in that.'

Alex nods. 'We talk to Mr Clarke about it first?' He raises his eyebrows to the other two and they grin. 'Let's do some research at school about recycling plastic.'

Alex and Bonnie check out the library at lunch. It's a community one, so adults from the town or district are often in there, especially with preschool kids, but Alex finds a vacant computer booth designated for students. He types in *recycling plastic*.

'Incredible.' Bonnie blows a breath at the long list of results that appears. 'How do we choose?'

'We start at the top.'

After ten minutes they have lots of notes about coasters made of tightly wound coloured plastic bags, jewellery from old plastic, mats made out of plastic rope. 'That would be good for the blue plastic twine that holds hay bales together,' Alex says. 'We've got coils of it from when I feed out the hay.'

Then they find the word *transmutation*. And photos of plastic bowls and bread boards. 'That's incredible,' Bonnie says. 'Look what they're made of.'

Alex scans the page. 'Plastic bread tags.' They watch a YouTube clip of a machine crushing the tags.

Bonnie turns to him. 'Kids could collect those tags. I wonder why they're not all made of cardboard now.'

'Bet they will one day. We could send the ones we collect to this place where they crush them.'

'What if we crush them ourselves and upcycle them into candle holders, or little bowls. That's what the club could be about: transmutation.'

Alex stares at her. 'You serious? One of those machines could cost forty grand.' He knows how expensive some of their farm machinery was. He hates the way he sounds like a damp rag. 'Even a second-hand one could be too much.' Mum used to say that when his dad wanted new machinery. Though right now Mum would say yes to anything Dad wanted. Alex types in *second-hand granulating machine*. A few items come up on eBay. The cheapest is nine thousand dollars. 'It's still a lot of money.'

'We could raise some.'

Alex is sceptical. People are reeling from a drought. Farmers can't even get a hay crop in and have to sell livestock before they want to for low prices.

Then Bonnie clicks on another link. 'Look at this!' she almost shouts. '*Partner with Transmutation and make an impact.*'

'Impact for what?'

'Like we were talking about on the bus. Helping the atmosphere and the environment.'

She scans the screen. 'See, here's a small business proposal suitable for towns or schools.'

Alex reads out, '*Three-in-one micro-recycler.*' Then he adds, '*Twelve grand.*'

The librarian, Ms Shultz, who doubles as their HASS teacher, comes over. 'You two sound excited.'

That would be Bonnie, Alex thinks.

'We want to upcycle plastic into other useful items,' Bonnie says. 'It's called transmutation. It lowers carbon emissions to help the atmosphere.'

'Making a new thing from an old,' Ms Shultz murmurs. She opens up another tab. 'Have a look at this website. At times quick-response government grants for small projects are available for rural areas doing it tough. See what it says about recycling and the environment.'

Bonnie takes over the mouse and by the time the end-of-lunch bell rings, they have guidelines and a form printed out to fill in later.

'Maybe this could be a small business for the school,' Bonnie says. 'The transmutation people even sell re-usable water bottles. We can help like they do.'

Alex can't imagine it, but he doesn't want to wipe that glow off Bonnie's face. 'C'mon, we'll be late for class.'

Mr Clarke is on bus duty that afternoon at the bus stop and they tell him all about it. Bonnie gives him the forms they printed off. 'I can help with this,' he says. 'I've had some experience with applying for grants. We'll need to write a proposal. What do you want me to say?'

'Everything we just told you.' Bonnie's so excited she's almost hopping.

'You think twelve thousand dollars is enough?'

Alex gives him the transmutation website address. 'We saw a package online for that,' Alex says. But he's thinking the money might be better spent buying in hay for the whole district.

'Okay.' Mr Clarke's eyes are shining. 'I'll check it out with the principal, Mr Wanganeen, and the Governing Council. The SRC, too. If they all think it's a good idea, I'll submit this ASAP.'

'Thank you, Mr Clarke.' Bonnie looks like she could hug him.

Fifteen

Harry, Bonnie and Alex have decided that Mr Clarke should tell the school about the project. Since Harry and Alex know a few of the older girls have it in for Bonnie, they don't want them to think she's too big for her boots and make it worse. No one likes a person coming into a district telling everyone what to do better.

Mr Clarke has done his own research. 'This transmutation project is a great idea. An activity all the kids can get involved in if they want to, either collecting plastics, sorting them, or making their own upcycled crafts. Creative and great for the environment. And, the principal and Parents and Friends Association think it's a good idea too.' Bonnie beams at him.

'Have you got a name for the group?' Mr Clarke asks.

Bonnie hesitates. 'I like what you just said: the Transmutation Project.'

'Yeah,' Alex agrees. 'That sounds more exciting than an upcycling club.'

'I like Recycle Club,' Harry says. 'I reckon the little kids would enjoy it.'

'Okay,' Mr Clarke says, 'the kids can vote at the first meeting. You still fine with me announcing the project, Bonnie? I hear it was your idea.'

'We all helped.' She just looks happy it's going to happen.

At assembly Kris tells everyone about a sharing group he's starting for adults to talk about the drought and how it is affecting their family. 'Talking about an event or issue helps us more than we realise. Details are online. Don't forget to tell your dads and big brothers that when they have time the Men's Shed is available for projects and sharing too. At the moment Mr Frost is working on restoring an FJ Holden at the shed and anyone over eighteen is welcome to help with that.'

Alex pricks up his ears. His dad likes machines and engines.

Sophie gets up next to speak on behalf of the SRC. 'Hi, everyone. Mr Clarke has told me about a special upcycling project to help our environment and I'm happy to say that the SRC is excited for this to go ahead.' Bonnie grins at Alex and Harry.

Mr Clarke speaks about transmuting plastics. 'Please come to the first session on Wednesday to discuss this project. The Year Sevens will run it and explain the Transmutation Project.' Alex thinks that should keep the heat off Bonnie and her camels. Then Mr Clarke mentions the grant. 'I feel hopeful that we'll receive funds for this.'

Alex feels a flutter in his gut. Was it wise to mention the grant? Many people are in need because of the drought. Everyone in the region, never mind Summer and Tara, could think of a better use of funds. He looks around. He can see Tara, but not Summer.

Bonnie and the younger kids start collecting suitable recyclables from home and neighbours like a rogue ram is charging them. They need materials so there'll be an activity for the little kids to do for the first session, while the bigger kids can discuss what they'd like to develop with the Transmutation Project. In a school as small as theirs, they're used to all ages doing the same activity, just at different levels of difficulty.

Wednesday lunchtime arrives. The meeting is held in the art studio where they have art lessons with Ms Penna. All the lower primary kids come and most of the Years Three to Sixes. Sophie is there but not Summer or Tara. Alex is not surprised. Josh in Year Twelve can't attend as he's often working online across breaks, but he says it's a great project to be involved in. Benjamin, the Year Eleven student, arrives a bit late. He seems very interested. 'I might be able to use this for my research project,' he says.

They end up with twenty-five kids. 'Most of the school,' Alex says. Mr Clarke and Kris walk in just before it starts.

Alex shows them the video of the transmutation machine working.

One of the little kids asks about crafts. 'We can do some other crafts too if you kids would like,' Bonnie says. Alex explains more about the package and how they need to choose a mould that will come with the machine. 'We'll be able to crush plastic and transmute it if we can get a three-in-one micro-recycling package.'

'This will rely on us getting a grant,' Harry says.

Sophie raises a hand. 'What about that money our community was given the year before last when the governments officials came to visit drought-stricken areas and we had the fete? The Recovery of Regional Areas grant? The Men's Shed received help from that for a project. There might be some left. We could apply for a strategic business grant – it could still involve the trans-mutation package, but it could be a job provider based at the school. That way the whole community is involved and the kids at school are still helping. Like, won't you need more money than the amount of the package to pay for other expenses?'

Alex sees Kris writing in a notebook. Sophie has made a good point. No wonder she's on the SRC.

'Let's vote,' Harry says. 'Who thinks this project is a great idea?' Most of the kids raise their hands. Some shout 'Yes!'

'Okay,' Alex says. 'Looks like we have a Transmutation Project. Now we need to vote on what to make first. The machine uses a mould like biscuit cutters or cake tins. If we bake a cake in a heart-shaped tin, the cake turns out a heart shape. So we have to tell the machine what to make by using a mould.' He pulls up the website on his laptop again. 'We can make doorknobs, combs, rulers, handles, bowls, bread boards. If we want to make a different item later, then we can ask Transmutation to sell us another mould.'

Some of the younger kids say combs and rulers, but overall, most think bowls will be an easier item to sell. Sophie sums it up, 'Not everyone needs doorknobs, but everyone does need bowls and they'd make good gifts filled with baked goodies.' Everyone agrees to that. They decide on smaller bowls, until they collect more plastic.

While the older kids discuss it, the fifteen kids from lower primary start making recycled items like bookmarks and cards from scrap paper and cardboard. Bonnie shows other kids how to sort different types of plastics into cardboard boxes ready for when the machine comes. Sophie squeezes paint onto palettes so she can show kids how to do dot paintings on tiles that she found going to waste in their shed. 'For coasters,' she says.

Alex likes Sophie's idea about the finance. Being a business for the school with community help and giving people a job would go down better in the district.

He hopes they get the funds, otherwise all these kids will be disappointed – as well as Bonnie.

At the end of lunch Sophie puts the paints away. 'This Transmutation Project is cool, Bonnie.' She grins at Alex and Harry too. 'It's what our Yura ancestors always taught,' she raises her eyebrows at Harry and he nods, 'to look after our place, look after country. You take bushfires – they were never as bad as they are now, because my gran says her great-grandfather used to burn off in the winter. And they grew the right plants for the soil. This upcycling of plastic is doing a good thing too.'

Bonnie's nodding. 'Thanks, Sophie.'

Bonnie gets off the bus at Alex's place after school. 'How about we sort your plastic recycling into boxes ready to take to school? You could bring them on the bus one at a time. I'm doing it at our place, too.'

Alex takes her around the back of the machinery shed.

'We can use plastic bottles and containers that food or liquid come in. Even plastic bags make a carbon foot-print when lots are weighed together.'

When they have collected enough cardboard boxes of items to take to school for the project, Bonnie picks up her backpack. 'Let's sit in your garden. Are you coming, Tangi?' Tangi barks once.

'I reckon that's a yes.' Alex pats her.

He brings a rug and spreads it out near the herb garden. Tangi sits by Bonnie and smiles at her with her tongue lolling out.

Bonnie laughs and hugs her. 'You look really happy today, Tangi. What's up?'

Alex blurts out, 'It's because you're here.' *Ouch*. His face grows hot as she smiles widely at him.

'Summer wasn't at school again today,' he says to take the heat off himself, but Bonnie doesn't bite.

Just nods and opens her backpack. 'I have a gift for you and Tangi.'

He's intrigued. 'No way?'

Bonnie has a private smile like that ancient painting in Europe called the *Mona Lisa*. She pulls a package out of her backpack and hands it to him. Alex can't remember when he's had a surprise like this. He fumbles with the string, but finally undoes it. Bonnie doesn't tell him to hurry. He pulls out four little boots. They look a bit like miniature Ugg boots made out of tan leather with laces to tie them on. They wouldn't even fit on his big toes and he raises his eyebrows at Bonnie, like, *what's this?*

'After you told me Tangi's story, I started to think. Then when we checked the tanks, I could see she can't walk far. Sophie helped me make these boots. Her mum's a nurse at the hospital in town and knew about them.'

Alex holds them up – they're light, maybe Tangi could wear them. 'Thank you, it's—' He stops at the evident care behind the gift. It makes him blink. 'That's the kindest thing . . .' He tells Tangi to sit. 'Now, Tangi, these boots are made for walking so you can come with us when we ride.' He puts one on, ties the leather thong around the boot and her leg and Tangi whimpers. Bonnie pats her to keep her from licking or biting it off.

He puts on the others until she has all four tied on. 'No one will be able to tell where the boots start and your legs finish, eh?' Tangi bites at the knot. 'Ah-ah, no, Tangi.' She sits still at his admonishment. 'Looks like you'll need some practice in them.'

Bonnie giggles. 'You look so cute, Tangi.' She jumps

up and runs to the ghost gum. 'Catch me, girl.' It's a challenge Tangi can't refuse, and she's caught Bonnie long before she reaches the tree. 'Your boots are still on, Tangi. Well done.' Tangi walks around like there's a prickle under her tail, lifting her feet too high.

'You'll be an old hand at boots soon,' Bonnie says to Tangi. Alex nods. He'll have to put them on her every day for her to get used to them. 'You can get proper ones from the vet or online if these wear out,' Bonnie says.

When it's time to take Bonnie back home, he whistles for Jago. He comes cantering to the fence, dust flying behind him and his mane lifting.

'He's beautiful cantering like that,' Bonnie whispers.

'C'mon, Jago, we'll go for a ride, all four of us.' He opens the gate and Jago slips through. He says hello to Alex first, then to Bonnie by putting a lip on her face. She laughs. 'He kisses worse than a camel, so whiskery.' Alex grins as he puts the bridle on.

Alex mounts Jago. 'Jump, Tangi.' She runs and jumps as Alex catches her. Then he pulls Bonnie up behind him.

She puts her arms around Alex's waist. 'Hope you don't mind,' she says. 'I want to stay on.'

'Nah, no problem.' He tries not to think about it, but warmth courses right through him. They canter across the southern paddock, walk up Rocky Peak, Jago whinnying his pleasure and Tangi grinning, then down the other side. If only the ride would never end.

Sixteen

||||||||||||||||||||||||||||||||||||||||||||||||||||||||||||||||||||||||||||||

At assembly the following Friday, Mr Clarke says, 'As you know the Year Sevens are piloting the Transmutation Project, the making of new plastic items from old ones to reduce their carbon footprint. I submitted an application for a quick-response grant last week just in time before the grant round closed for the end of May, and the funding body notify successful applicants a week later.' Bonnie's eyes shine at Alex. He thinks he knows what's coming too. 'I am happy to announce that this morning I received the email notifying us that the grant application for the three-in-one micro-recycler machine has been successful. And now we can order it.'

Instant 'oohs' and 'aahs' emanate from the younger kids. The Year Fives and Sixes stand up, start clapping and shout, 'Yes!' Harry gives a kookaburra call and Mr Clarke almost loses everyone's attention.

'That's not all.' Kris stands and manages to make himself heard above the noise.

The kids quieten down. 'Sophie mentioned the grant the community received the year before last, and I drove down to the district council to ask about the Transmutation Project. They're keen about the concept and recognise what it will do for the school and our community. However, they stipulate that a person needs to supervise the project and act as the go-between with the school and district council. Also, we need a person who can supervise the use of the machinery and provide maintenance. It will be a paid job for those people a day or two a week. If we can provide their names, the council will support us to pay for these two community roles. If you know anyone who would be interested, please tell me.'

Alex wonders if Kris is looking at him when he says that last bit. Seems like Kris knows more about his dad than Alex thought.

Alex comes in early for lunch from the shed the next day and finds Dad ready at the table with a cuppa. Dad's had a string of happier days now, and Alex has been thinking about Kris's plea. This might be a good time to get his dad interested. He brings his laptop out from his room and opens it. 'I've got something to show you, Dad.'

The internet connection takes a while, so his dad finishes his coffee. Finally, the site appears. 'This is called a transmutation machine.' Alex clicks the video on the site and makes it full screen. His dad leans forward to watch.

Afterwards, Alex says, 'This bloke made the first machines from old ovens and microwaves. Transmutation helps the environment as it reduces the impact of plastic by recycling the plastic we already have that otherwise ends up as landfill.' His dad hasn't commented yet. Alex takes a punt. 'His main ideas involve sustainability, craftsmanship, community and innovation—'

'Sustainability is always important,' Dad says, moving the laptop closer so he can work the trackpad. It's what we need to do on this place. Craftsmanship and creativity, too – there is always a way to fix a machine.'

Alex grins as his dad navigates the site.

'Down in Robe, eh?'

'Yeah.'

'Local, then.'

Alex grins – it's over seven hours' drive to Robe, down on the Limestone Coast, but he's not about to argue. 'You could say that.'

'Wouldn't mind seeing a machine that a bloke's put together like this.'

Alex tries to speak casually. 'The school's getting one. When it comes, shall we go and see it?'

'Good-oh. They might need help with that.'

Alex sees a movement in his peripheral vision – his mum, wiping her eyes.

It's Sunday afternoon and Alex is in the shed using the welder when Bonnie appears at his side. He gives a start and pushes up his visor. 'You gave me a fright. Where's Ruby?'

'On the other side of the shed where Jago is – and he's not snorting.'

He grins at that. 'You didn't look at the flash, did you? You don't have goggles on.'

Bonnie shakes her head. 'Dad uses a welder too, so I know not to. But your mum sent me down here. She didn't warn me.'

'She doesn't know what I'm doing.'

'Oh?'

'I'm making her a birthday gift.'

'That's incredible, Alex.'

'Don't let on.' He feels exposed, but he needn't have worried.

'As if. How come you can weld?'

'Dad.' It's all Alex can say. What he says and what he thinks are like oil and vinegar. That one word conjures up the Easter holidays last year when his dad decided to teach him how to weld. He just feels bad for wishing his dad was still like that.

'You okay?' Bonnie's staring at him.

'Yeah. Let me show you.' He turns the steel structure around.

'Oh,' Bonnie says, 'you do bush art.'

'Is that what it's called?'

'Yep. It's better than those mass-produced bush animals.' Bonnie's eyes gleam. 'This is creative.'

Alex shrugs. 'I just use stuff that's lying around.' He points to the triangular pieces layered down the back. 'These are plough discs. They called them ploughshares.'

'This is huge.' Bonnie picks up a horseshoe from the bench. 'So heavy.'

'Clydesdales. My great-grandfather loved his horses, Mum said. They couldn't work two days straight, so they bred a lot of them. Fifty. That's why there are so many horseshoes around.'

'That many must have been wonderful to see.' Bonnie walks along the bench and checks out his materials. She picks up a steel ring. 'What's this for?'

'Harness.'

'And these old chains?'

'Off the machinery. Plough, probably.'

She picks up a piece of blue crockery. 'This is willow pattern. Mum loves this. You use this too?'

He tries to ignore her reference to her mum. 'Yeah – either I'll drill a hole through a piece or glue it in. A bit of blue crockery looks good on rusty steel.'

'Good for eyes?'

'Maybe. I find pieces when I'm digging in the garden. In the old days they buried all their rubbish near the house. I found most of this at the ruins of my great-grandparents' place.'

Bonnie comes to stand by him. 'Alex.' She waits until he's looking at her. Her eyes are huge. 'You're already doing it.'

'Doing what?'

'What we've been talking about – upcycling, re-using, reducing the rubbish. You're creating a new thing out of old things! Isn't that transmutation?'

Alex doesn't know what to say. 'I'm just making a gift.'

Bonnie grins. 'Sure you are. But you're also helping the environment in a beautiful way. You're talented, Alex.'

Alex can feel his neck growing hot. He'd better not be blushing. 'How do you know so much about art?'

'My mum's an artist. She's teaching me to draw.'

Alex stares at her. 'Your mum?' He doesn't want to sound annoyed, but he can't stop it. 'Why do you always say that?' Then he says the cruellest thing. 'She's dead.'

Bonnie's eyes widen as her mouth falls open.

Alex's stomach drops through the floor. 'I'm sorry, I shouldn't have said that.' He tries saying what he should have in the first place. 'What art do you like doing besides drawing?'

'Sewing.' But she's not looking at him anymore. Why couldn't he keep his mouth shut?

They visit Asmaan and Gertrude, but Bonnie doesn't say much. It's like her light has been snuffed out. Alex could kick himself.

His mum is home and she asks Bonnie to stay for dinner. They cook together. Alex cuts silverbeet from his garden. Dad even joins them at the table. Bonnie talks mainly to his mum and dad. She hardly glances at Alex. 'You should come and see the eagle, Rachael.' She turns to Tom. 'She loves the aviary Alex helped Sully and Pop with.'

Alex eases out a slow breath. She's mentioned him, maybe it's okay now. His dad nods at Bonnie. There's a whisper of a grin on his face.

'Alexander says you have a joey too?' Rachael asks.

'Yep, she's doing well. Starting to jump higher. Soon she'll be over the garden fence. She got her front legs stuck in Pop's trousers on the line yesterday, like she thought they were a sack for her to dive into, but Mum didn't mind.' Bonnie says the last bit like she didn't mean to. She glances at Alex and he wishes he could turn back the clock.

Alex looks at his mum. Her mouth is slightly open – is that surprise? Why does Bonnie say her mum is still alive? He thinks about it some more. She doesn't actually say her mum is alive, just gives the impression she is. Is there a difference?

They take dessert out to the veranda and watch the sunset. Alex never gets tired of it, even though he sees it every day. Tonight, there's a mass of purple and a strip of yellow on the horizon. The purple changes to pink fingers stroking the sky. It's better than projection illuminart on silos.

His mum tells a story about tourists at the pub. 'I think this couple had never been up here before. They asked for an outback platter, but when they saw it had emu mettwurst, kangaroo sausage and slices of roast goat they complained. Said it was cruel to our native animals, and where was the famous beef we're supposed to have up here. They must think goats are native because they run wild. Wonder what they would have said about camel steaks. Sorry, Bonnie.'

'No worries. I like my joey but I'll still eat kangaroo, to save on having beef.' Bonnie describes how they capture the feral camels. 'There are regulations for the musters and culls,' she says. 'So it's done right with no cruelty. Animal Welfare has posted the way it should be done – camels get stressed quickly. They're usually quite timid, even though they're big.'

'What sort of rules?' Dad asks. Alex tries not to look surprised at his dad joining in. His mum is watching Tom as if she doesn't know whether to be happy or wary.

Bonnie pauses a moment. 'To not push them too fast if mustering – use sheep dogs, not cattle dogs. Use transportable yards so they don't have to travel so far. To not muster pregnant animals or mothers with calves. They must have a camel handler on the team. If they are culling, only an experienced operator can shoot them. Often they're mustered for meat, but many live camels are exported, like to the Middle East. We try to get up there before the culling season starts, to catch the younger ones.'

Alex's dad changes the subject. 'Alex says the school transmutation machine is your idea.'

Bonnie looks surprised. 'We both saw it online at the same time.'

'But she ran with the idea,' Alex says. 'And now we have a grant to buy it.'

Her eyes twinkle at him and he knows she's letting go of the tension from before. Then she says, 'Tom, would you like to be involved in that?'

Alex holds his breath. Talk about taking the bull by the horns – he was going to wait a bit before he went that far. His mum fidgets with her earring.

'It sounds interesting. Let me know when it comes. I'll have a look and then we'll see.' Bonnie can sure charm his dad. It's like Bonnie fills the hole that Lily's left in some ways.

'Okay.' Bonnie's eyes shine at him, then she switches that gaze to Alex. If anything, it's brighter.

The sound of a ute crawling up the rise to the house makes Tangi lift her head, but she doesn't bark.

'It's Sully,' Bonnie says. 'Thank you so much for tea, Rachael. See you later, Tom.' She kisses Dad on the cheek. He actually smiles.

Sully swings out of the front seat. Alex thinks how his dad used to move effortlessly like that. Tangi stands. 'It's okay, girl,' Alex says. Tangi looks at him as if to say she knows already. Just doing her job.

'G'day, Rachael, Tom, Alex.' Sully tips his hat as he reaches the veranda. 'Thanks for having Bonnie over.'

Dad nods at him.

'Thanks for letting her stay,' Rachael says. 'She's a treasure.'

Sully grins. 'We think she's special too.'

So does Alex, but he doesn't dare say it.

'Cup of coffee, Sully?' There's a positive note in his mum's voice.

'No, thank you, better be getting back to Pop. Don't like to leave him alone in the evening.'

Alex glances at Bonnie, but she says nothing about her mum being home or not. She thanks them before collecting her backpack and hopping in the ute. She waves at Alex. 'See ya on the bus.'

'Sure.'

They drive slowly out to the road, tying Ruby's reins to the tow bar on the way like last time.

After his dad heads for the bedroom, Alex helps his mum clear the table. 'Bonnie talks about her mum freely,' she comments.

He nods, pausing in his packing of the dishwasher.

Rachael watches him. 'I heard it's just Sully, his grandfather and Bonnie who live there. But I must have heard wrong. Have you met her mother?'

Alex loads the cutlery into the basket with particular care. 'Never.' Then he stands up. 'There's something Pop said that I can't make out.'

'Can you tell me what it is?'

'I think so. He said Bonnie's mum died in a car accident when Bonnie was a kid. But then she said today that her mum is an artist.' He eyeballs his mum. 'She said *is*. And that thing about the joey getting into clothes on the line . . .'

His mum wrinkles her forehead. 'Is she in denial about her mum dying?'

'She doesn't seem that sort of person.' He wants to say she's strong, resilient and wise.

'Maybe she believes her mum is alive in heaven. That's how I think of my parents.'

'You don't talk about them in the present tense, though.'

His mum pauses. 'No, that would be misleading.' She pours water from the kettle into the sink to wash the saucepans, since the kitchen hot water takes a while. 'Alexander, I'm sure she'll tell you. Just give her time.' She smiles at him gently, and he remembers how hard he finds it to open up to anyone about his dad.

Seventeen

Alex takes off his jeans jacket and hangs it on a post. He thought he'd need it this afternoon since winter has begun, but, no, it's still warm, especially when he's digging a garden bed near his herb garden and veggie patch. The ground is so hard that he'll have to soak it with precious water to even make this work.

He stops to wipe the perspiration from his face with his arm. His heart's not in it, and he puts the pick away in the shed. Maybe one day it will rain, and Dad will be like he used to be, and Bonnie will tell him about her mum.

Alex heads inside for a cool drink and notices his mum at the sink where she could always see his dad coming in from the machinery shed. He fills a glass from the fridge. 'Do you think Dad's getting better?'

His mum doesn't answer his question, just carries on peeling spuds. She's getting as glum as Dad lately. Alex thinks how much fun they've always had cooking together, telling jokes, how she'd flick him with the tea towel. At times it's like someone sadder has taken over her body.

'Why don't we talk more about Dad's illness?' Alex persists.

That's when Mum flies at him. It's so random he gapes at her.

'You don't understand,' she shouts. 'You're thirteen years old. You don't know what it's like trying to borrow money, pleading with the bank, keeping sheep alive, trying to make the farm sustainable, what's it's like to have to do everything—'

Doesn't he? He knows about filling in for his dad. But it isn't the right time to say, so he retreats to the garden.

There are no weeds to pull, so he sits with Tangi at his feet. She gives his hand a lick. 'Thanks, Tangi, you're the best friend. I'm woeful at comforting Mum.' It's like they're two show horses taking a jump from either side and clashing in the middle. His mum does have her moments, though, when Bonnie, Sully or Roger comes over or when she hugs him and tells him she loves him. He hopes she never decides he's too old for that.

Mum comes out while he's collecting eggs. 'I'm sorry, Alexander. I don't know what came over me. It's just so difficult keeping it all together.'

He nods. 'It's okay, Mum. I know it's hard.'

She sits beside him. 'Feeling depressed and anxious can not only make people sad and tired, but angry too. Remember it's the depressive feelings barking, and not your dad. Same with me.' She goes on, 'You're such a helpful son—' and then bursts into tears.

Alex isn't sure what to do. Should he hug her? His dad would have before he became ill. He puts his arm around her. Mum's eyes are red, but she tries to smile through the tears. 'This is why I don't like to talk – I don't want you to see me like this. I'm meant to be an adult and I wish I didn't feel like the only one here.' Her voice breaks again.

'I don't mind if you cry, Mum.' Alex doesn't say that's why he stays quiet too, but now he's wondering if crying is better than saying nothing at all.

Alex doesn't sleep well. He hears his dad sobbing in the night, and his voice, sounding cracked. 'I can't do this anymore, Rach. I can't get those sheep out of my head.' Then his mum's murmuring. He can imagine her stroking his dad's head like she used to stroke his, Alex's, when he was a kid.

And yet Alex thought Dad was getting better. Living with his dad is like riding a brumby – lots of ups and downs and falling off at the end with a bump. As he drifts off to sleep again he imagines his dad's tears flowing out like a fire hose into the dam paddock, flooding it with water, washing away all the bones and all the pain.

In the morning Alex gets up with a groan. He must have slept a bit, but his head is full of wool. He manages to feed the animals and collect eggs, but Tangi can't coax him to smile, nor can Jago when he pushes his bottom lip out and blows in Alex's face. Even Bonnie's chatter on the bus doesn't cheer him up.

At morning recess, he hears Tara telling Summer about the Transmutation Project. 'Recycling is good,' Tara says. 'I mean, we have to do everything we can so our kids will have a planet.'

'There are other ways to help,' Summer says. 'Money for a plastic-crushing machine? Huh. How about a loan for paying off farm machinery or for hay? A job for someone?' Then she sees Bonnie and says louder, 'Those camels will end up drinking all the water in the district, since the Salehs will have to cart water for them.' Whoa, Summer is sure back at school.

Tara scoffs. 'They're only good for camel rides, but how can that help the community?'

'They'll run rampant down the road and break everyone's fences and attack everyone's dogs.'

Alex frowns. So *everyone* knows about Asmaan killing a feral dog now? As Alex strides over to Summer, he ignores the voice in his head that says, *Stop right now. Calm down.* Bonnie's quiet, urgent 'Alex?' doesn't stop him, either.

'What would you know, Summer?' He doesn't even wait until he's close enough to speak at normal volume. 'You live in town. Water comes to you, your internet works every day, you don't have to rely on a satellite dish for coverage, you don't have electricity cuts that mean you need to use a generator to save the food in the freezer.'

Summer stares at him, her mouth half open. He expects she'll be angry, and he's ready for that. But he's not ready for the look of naked desolation on her face.

Alex closes his eyes. He's upsetting everyone lately.

Summer returns her mouth back to normal, covers up her animosity. 'In case you don't know, Dad was a farmer, but we had to sell up. He got more money for the farm machinery than the land that he'd lived on all his life, and his dad before him. *You* should know what that feels like.' With horror Alex sees the tears form in her eyes, but she doesn't dash them away.

He feels gutted with shame, but he wants to stand up for Bonnie. He opens his mouth to speak. Summer beats him to it.

'Your dad is a farmer,' she says steadily.

Any compassion he felt vanishes. 'Keep my dad out of it.' It comes out as a shout. He doesn't want to do this anymore.

Alex pushes his way out of the classroom and to the oval. He's really blown it now. Even Bonnie doesn't come after him.

Kris does, though. In their school, there's no arguing without everyone knowing. Most of the school was there. 'Hey, mate.'

Alex glances up. 'I don't want to talk about it.'

'That's fine.' Kris sits cross-legged beside him in the dirt. Five minutes go by.

Alex clears his throat. Kris probably won't leave until he starts talking – he just needs to keep off the topic of Dad. 'I didn't know Summer's dad had it so bad. She lives in town. I didn't even know her before we ended up in the same class this year, so I just thought . . .' He doesn't know what he thought.

Kris glances at him, waits awhile. 'The town kids have suffered from the drought too, not just you kids on properties.'

'That sucks.'

'You bet.'

'I thought they had it pretty good.'

'Summer's father has to do any job he's offered.'

'Bummer.' So all that superiority she shows is just a cover-up. How does he come across? Like he's holding it all together? Like he doesn't mind doing his dad's work after school and on weekends, because Dad isn't well enough to do it?

He glances at Kris patiently waiting, staring at the cobalt sky dominating the landscape. It won't do any good talking to Kris. How can he help? Alex stands up to head back to class.

Then Kris says, 'Keep your dad talking, find something creative he's interested in. Don't give up. It will help.'

How many people know his dad isn't coping? Alex turns back to Kris. 'Thanks.' He hesitates, then says, 'I showed Dad the video of the transmutation machine.' Kris watches him like Bonnie does, no pressure. 'It's the first thing he's been interested in for ages. I'm not sure if I can promise anything – he's up and down a lot,' he breathes out, 'but when the machine comes, can Dad come in to see it?'

Kris stands too and puts a hand on Alex's shoulder. 'That would be great, Alex. Even if your dad doesn't want to be involved, just having him interested must be very encouraging for you and your mum. Come by my office before you leave. I have a book I think you'd like to read. It's called *Living with a Black Dog*.'

Confused, Alex thinks of Tangi. 'I already know how to live with a black dog.'

Kris grins at him. 'Not that sort of dog. You'll see.'

Intrigued, Alex drops by Kris's office before afternoon classes start. Kris gives him a book in a paper bag.

Later in class, Alex thinks about what Summer said. *Your dad is a farmer*. What was she getting at? It didn't sound like an accusation, so why did he lose it?

Before bed, Alex looks at the book Kris lent him. It has a colour picture on each page and he soon learns that 'black dog' is a metaphor for depression. It's easy to read, and he can see his family on every page. Even the picture of a guy feeling depressed looks like Dad, often unshaven, dragging his feet, wearing shabby old clothes. Then a page stops him in his tracks. The words flash at him like neon lights. *Depression is an illness, not a weakness*. Has he been thinking less of his dad because he's ill?

Just as he gets into bed his phone pings. It's a message from Lily.

You OK, Alex?

Had a fight with Summer

She sends a commiserating emoji.

She's sensitive, takes things hard.

Alex thinks how bad he would feel having to leave home.

And you, Lil?

Sigh. I'm missing the property. All my memories are there.

Alex is quick to reply.

Growing up in a drought isn't great

No but we were together.

Alex lays his phone on the desk. Lily's admission reminds him of Summer. Maybe she's feeling like his dad. Alex knows how lost he would feel if he had to leave Spring Park.

Eighteen

A week later, before class begins Mr Clarke tells the Year Sevens to go to the unused classroom next to the art studio at lunchtime. 'Take your laptop, Alex.' Then he smiles. 'Kris says your father may like to come, if he's free.'

'What d'you think it is?' Bonnie whispers.

'The machine?'

'Really?' Bonnie's eyes shine. It's good to see.

Alex rings his mum at recess to see if Roger could bring Dad to school – he knows Roger's working with him on the property today, so it could be great timing. 'Remind Dad what he said, Mum, about wanting to see the machine when it came.'

'Okay, I'll try.'

By the time the Year Sevens arrive, Mr Clarke and Mr Wanganeen are in the room chatting. On a long table is a huge cardboard box.

A minute later, Roger enters, along with Alex's dad. Dad is in his old trackpants and his hair's messy, but at least he shaved yesterday.

They all stare at the box.

'Incredible,' Bonnie whispers. She reads the print on the box aloud: *'Three-in-one micro-recycler.'*

Kris walks in then. 'G'day everyone. Let's get cracking, shall we?'

They carefully pull open the packaging and find the three parts of the machine: the shredder, the injector and the extruder. Mr Clarke hands over the assembly instructions to Alex's dad.

'Tom, would you like to read this and then get the machine set up? If it's too much in one go you can take the notes home to study and we can put it together another time. You can ring Transmutation if there's any problem.' He points to a phone number.

Alex holds his breath; there was a time when saying that to Dad would have been a challenge. He hopes Dad feels up to it. There's a video, so Alex pulls out his laptop and they all watch it first.

'It doesn't look that complicated,' his dad comments.

Bonnie says, 'We're going to need a sign outside the library that says to bring all your clean plastic. We've already got tubs to sort the different plastics.'

'We'll need containers with lids to put all the shredded plastic in,' Alex says.

'There's a lot of plastic buckets with lids hanging around at the station my dad works on,' Harry says. 'I can bring those.'

'You'll need a container underneath the shredder too,' Alex points out, 'to catch the plastic flakes. Do we need to cut a hole in the table?' He glances at Mr Wanganeen.

'Do whatever you have to do – this isn't one of our new tables.'

'I'll head off to the Men's Shed,' Roger says, 'for tools.'

'Interesting.' Alex's dad sounds more animated than he has for ages, and Alex's spirits rise. Maybe this is what Kris meant about having something creative for his dad to do. He hopes it helps.

The bell rings. 'You go,' his dad says. 'After school, come back and get me before the bus goes. I'll come home with you if Roger has to leave.' He gives Alex the ghost of a grin.

As they walk back to class Bonnie says, 'I think your dad likes it.'

Alex is still feeling the warm effects of that almost-grin. 'Yeah, I reckon he does.'

Bonnie goes off to join Sophie, and Harry says, 'Has your old man been sick, mate?'

Alex thinks about the Black Dog book and nods. It's best to talk about it or it grows bigger, the book says. 'Yeah. I didn't say cos—' He can't continue. Why didn't he tell Harry? Because he was ashamed or just didn't know what to say? 'He's been sick since the bushfire, the sheep . . . you know?'

'Yeah. We know a bloke like that too. Must be hard, mate.' Harry makes it seem normal, and Alex catches himself. Of course his dad is normal – he's just got an illness, not a weakness. It feels good that Harry understands. They bump their fists together. Alex knows he won't have to explain it to Harry if he doesn't want to. That's what mates are for – to catch you when you fall.

When they return after class the machine is already assembled and Dad's having a cup of coffee.

'You've done it!' Alex says. 'You've even sawn a hole to let the shredded plastic through.'

Bonnie runs a hand over the triangular shredder. 'Tom, could you come back to the Transmutation Project on Wednesday and show everyone how it works?'

There's a glint in his father's eye that Alex hasn't seen for ages. 'Hmm,' he says. 'I'll give it a shot.'

At Wednesday lunchtime Roger brings Dad to school again. After signing in, Ms Shultz leads them to the Transmutation Project Room. That's what it's called now. All the kids are sitting on the carpet, just staring at the machine on the table. Even Benjamin, the Year Eleven student, is present. 'I've got permission to use this for my research project.' He looks as excited as Bonnie.

When his dad walks in Alex sucks in a breath. Dad's hair is cut, he's shaved and is wearing clean jeans. He gives the kids a quick smile. 'Shall we try to make it work?'

What a question. The kids get so noisy Sophie has to say, 'Shush!'

Alex's dad pushes down a switch on the machine. 'Can someone bring me three coloured plastic bottles, please?'

To stop a stampede, Alex beckons to Freddy to choose from a box of shampoo bottles. Freddie takes three over to the machine. 'Pop one in the shredder here.' Alex's dad points to the square, funnel-like machine. All the kids stand as one, craning to see.

'Come closer,' Alex says, 'but remember it is a machine, so be careful. No pushing.'

No one wants to miss out, so they fall quiet, listening to the crunch and rattle of the plastic being shredded by the blades. The flakes of plastic drop into a container under the table. The little kids point at it fluttering down like confetti.

Tom switches off the shredder and presses a button for heat. He shows the students the bowl mould and screws it on the end of the low, long part of the machine. 'This barrel is called the injection machine.'

As his father pulls down on a long lever to push the plastic through the heated barrel, Alex explains, 'The shredded plastic goes into this upside-down triangular part of the machine and it will get pushed into the mould as it is heated.'

When a small bowl, the same green colour as the shampoo bottles, is turned out of the mould, the kids let out a long 'Ooooh'. Dad's grin is wider than Alex has seen for over a year.

Kris takes photos with his phone while Bonnie grabs Alex's hand. 'It works, it works!'

Nineteen

||||||||||||||||||||||||||||||||||||||||||||||||||||||||||||||||||||||||||

Alex is eating his omelette on Sunday morning when he hears his mum's phone ring. She picks up, walking out to the veranda for better coverage. He hears her initial tone of horror, then calming comments of concern. What's happening? There's a silence before she comes into the kitchen.

She sits at the table in front of him and he stops eating. 'Alex, I have some news.'

'What's wrong? Not Lily? Grandad?'

She shakes her head. 'Summer Holding is missing. That was her mum.'

He'd never have imagined that. '*Missing?* How?'

'She went riding – Deb doesn't know if she's with anyone or not.'

Alex thinks how Summer's been absent from school a bit lately, and how she hasn't seemed happy when she's around.

'Ginger, her horse, came back in the night and the police won't search yet – they say she could be on her way home.'

'But she could have fallen.'

'She's a good rider, but anyone can fall if the horse is spooked,' Mum agrees.

Doesn't he know it. Falling off Jago that day on Rocky Peak could have been a lot worse if he'd been caught in a stirrup and dragged. 'Is her mum telling people in case they see her?'

'No. She remembered Tangi is a star muster dog – won those trials a few years ago. She can find lost sheep.'

'Summer's not a sheep, Mum. I can't take Tangi around to find Summer. It'd be like finding a needle in a haystack. In a good year.' He grins at his tacky drought joke.

'Alexander, her mum is beside herself. Says she has clothes that Summer wore yesterday for Tangi to sniff.'

Alex thinks. 'She's been out overnight. We need to narrow it down. If she rode from the outskirts of town where their house is – maybe a five to ten kay radius?' How will it be possible? He's a bit of a loner too, and he tries to see himself in Summer's shoes. If he'd lived on a property all his life and had to move to town, where would he ride to? It's a no-brainer.

He stands up so suddenly the chair topples. 'I reckon I know where she is. They lived on a property. It's not up this way or she would have been on our bus until last year.'

'Southwest of town.'

'Could you ask where?'

'Yes, but there's another thing.'

Alex looks at her expectantly.

'She mentioned the camels.'

'Camels? Summer's family hate them. She can't blame this on the camels.'

'No. Deb heard about Asmaan killing our feral dog.'

'What does she hope a camel will do?'

His mum shrugs. 'Maybe you would see better if you were riding one? And if there are feral dogs around? Deb's distraught and needs help.'

'Okay, I'll see what Sully thinks.' He runs his fingers through his hair while his mum calls Deb back.

She writes on scrap paper and gives it to Alex. 'Three Chain Road, number 180. The people who bought the place are away.'

That's probably why she went there, if his theory's right.

'It's a bigger place than ours, so it could take a while to find her.'

'What about being on their property without permission?'

'Deb will take responsibility.'

He makes the call to Sully.

Sully and Bonnie arrive within fifteen minutes with their camel truck. Sully tips his hat at Alex's mum. 'Rachael.'

'Thank you for coming,' she says. 'Deb Holding feels Summer may be in danger, and her husband is away fencing. I'm sorry Tom can't help, but Alexander will.'

Sully pushes his hat back. 'Camels are a good idea in a situation like this. Asmaan is the best one to take. Not only can he protect and kick, but he's tall – I'll see a lot from his back. And he has been known to find the odd goat or two that I've lost.'

Alex grins. 'A huge muster dog?'

'A muster camel, mate.'

They walk to the truck. Alex can see it's empty. 'You didn't bring Ruby?' He glances at Bonnie, but she gives him her massive smile. 'Gertrude would make an awful fuss if we took Asmaan and not her. You and I can ride her.'

'Okay.' Alex has only ridden Ruby, who is much smaller, and Bonnie held the reins. As long as he hangs on he should be fine. At least there are saddles in the truck.

Tangi is asking to come, her eyes and front paws showing how much she wants to. Alex isn't too sure. They may have a long way to ride. Then he remembers the little dog boots, and bends down to her. 'You can come if you wear your boots. Let's see if you can stand them for that long.'

Soon they're on the road, Tangi in the cabin with them. It's a half-hour to town, then Alex guides them the next five kays down the main road to Summer's old place. He hopes again he's right about where she went. She's old enough to have a boyfriend or girlfriend – what if she's just visiting them without her mum knowing and Ginger got away and ran home? He bets that's what the police think.

Alex opens the gate to the property and they drive through into a paddock. Sully unloads the groaning camels and tells them to kneel while he saddles them up. He shows Alex how to help.

'We'll split up,' Sully says, 'or we'll be here all day. If you find her, give a coo-ee and I hope I'm in earshot. Same with me. We'll meet back at the truck in three hours, even if we haven't found her. Three-thirty sharp. Okay?'

Sully turns to ride east on Asmaan while Alex and Bonnie set off south on Gertrude with Tangi tagging beside them. She's walking well with her boots on. Even runs off, sniffing stuff.

Bonnie hasn't said much. 'You okay?' he asks from behind her. Bonnie's not often this quiet.

'Just thinking.'

'What about?' Then he catches himself. 'Sorry.'

But she doesn't seem to mind. 'About how long it took for people to find Mum and me after the accident. We hit a roo, but we weren't on a main road. I was eight, and all I could think of was how hungry I was and how I wished Mum'd wake up and drive us back home.' Then she adds, 'I talk about my mum in the present tense because she's still alive, she's just not here. We'll see her again.'

Alex doesn't know what's best to say. 'You have Sully and Pop now.'

She half turns and he can see the beginnings of a smile on her face. 'Yep. I love them to bits, just sometimes I'd like to talk to a woman.'

'You can borrow my mum. She misses my sister, Lily.'

'I like Rachael, she's got a vibe.' Then Bonnie says, 'So are you okay about your dad?'

'It's hard at times. His moods go up and down, but it must be worse for him than us.'

166

Then she says, 'You know how Summer hasn't been at school much lately?'

'Yeah – I'm glad you haven't been getting teased as much, at least.'

'Maybe she's not feeling so well either.'

Alex thinks about that. 'It'd be a bummer having to sell your property.'

'If I lived here like Summer did I'd have a special place I'd want to go to,' Bonnie says. 'My special place is Rocky Peak, even though it straddles both our places.'

'Yeah, mine too.'

Tangi gives a bark and Alex scans the paddocks. 'Can't see anything like that here. Maybe a creek?'

There is nothing of interest in the first paddock. Gertrude has to kneel at each gate so Alex can get down to open it. Then she has to kneel again to let him on after he's shut it. It takes precious time and Jago might have been quicker, but at least Alex can see further on Gertrude.

In the next paddock there are a few steers and goats. The cattle are acting strange, all bunched up together in the southern corner opposite them like sheep that feel threatened. He doesn't mention it – no need to worry Bonnie, but he wonders what's spooked them.

Tangi heads off to check them out, but Alex calls to her. 'Tangi, get back here.' She takes a few seconds to obey. He can tell she senses something's wrong too.

'There's a line of red river gums,' Bonnie says, pointing east.

'Could be a creek.' They don't talk much in case Sully gives a *coo-ee*. Gertrude quickens her pace. This paddock is so dry it's like brown sand. In the distance to the north they see a whirly-whirly. 'Bet there's no water in the creek,' Alex says.

Gertrude is almost growling by the time they reach the tree line.

'She sounds upset,' Alex says. 'What's the matter?'

'Not sure. She's either scared or acting aggressive.'

Alex doesn't like the sound of either. Then Tangi barks in earnest.

They hear a cry.

Bonnie turns Gertrude's head towards the sound, further up the line of trees. But Gertrude must have heard it too – she falls into a run. Tangi bounds ahead. Alex hangs on to the saddle bar while Gertrude crashes through the trees. It is a creek, dry, but there's no time to think about that because they see Summer.

She's bailed up in a tree. Alex can see blood on her leg and her eyes are half shut. Tangi is racing towards the tree. And then Alex sees the danger.

'Tangi!' he shouts. 'No! Tangi, come back!' This time she doesn't listen.

Under Summer is a wild dog jumping up trying to catch her foot, which is slipping lower. Bonnie clicks to Gertrude to get closer, but Gertrude sidesteps. Alex watches Tangi, who's growling, her fur up. If she goes the wild dog she won't have much of a chance. When she was younger, she could be ferocious protecting the sheep, but now?

'We haven't got much time,' Alex says. 'Can Gertrude run the dog off? Kick it?'

'Asmaan's the kicker, but we can try.' Bonnie turns Gertrude's head towards the dog. She shies. Jago would have too. The dog is a mangy, snarling piece of work.

Bonnie pulls out a cane from her saddle and swipes Gertrude's side with it. 'Run! Run!'

Gertrude does a half-hearted rush at the dog, but halts just as Tangi reaches it. Tangi holds it up like it's a cantankerous ram, running from side to side and growling. The wild dog retreats from the tree, but not far enough to give them time to get Summer down. The dog circles, snarling at Tangi. It's not as big as the dog Asmaan killed, thinner, but it sure is mean. Same greyish colour as the one his mum shot.

Alex and Bonnie inch closer. 'Tangi, easy, girl.' If she goes for the dog he'll have to jump down. They can't risk getting the camel to kneel while the feral dog is there. 'I'll call Sully.' And he lets out a long *Cooo-eee*. They could do with Harry and his raucous cockatoo screech right now.

Summer groans. Bonnie stays quiet, but her back is tense.

The dog stands still, quivering, considering Gertrude, then locks its gaze on Tangi. The dog looks hungry. It glances up at Summer, its tongue protruding. It's bold like a fox, only bigger. Summer could fall. The dog would attack, but Tangi is between the tree and the wild dog, and her meaning is clear: to get the girl the feral dog has to go through her.

Suddenly Alex knows what's going to happen. 'Gimme that stick,' he says, and he takes it from Bonnie's hand. 'Tangi!' he shouts, at the same time the wild dog rushes her.

Alex jumps from Gertrude's back, rolls once and gets to his feet just as Bonnie kicks Gertrude into action. The dogs are a ball of growls and snarls. Alex reaches them a second before Gertrude. He hits the wild one with the cane and it growls at him. It's got Tangi round the neck and isn't letting go.

Then Gertrude acts. She kicks the wild dog with one leg, then the next – it's like she's dancing. The dog releases Tangi. Gertrude circles to kick it again, with two side legs at once. There's a high-pitched yelp and when Alex looks up, the dog is gone.

'Whoa, Gertrude, you're a ninja camel.'

Bonnie grins. 'They can even kick with four legs at once. I've never seen that, though.'

'Tangi, are you okay, girl?'

She tries to stand. Fortunately the bite hasn't drawn too much blood, but she's unsteady on her feet.

'Quick!' Bonnie says. 'Let's get Summer before that horrible dog comes back.'

Bonnie urges Gertrude to the tree. This time the camel is happy to comply. She stands still under the branch while Alex helps Summer down to sit in Bonnie's saddle. Bonnie has scooted closer to Gertrude's neck and twists to hold her upright. By Summer's wincing and sudden gasps, it seems like she's broken an ankle.

Alex checks all around. He can't see the wild dog. 'Bonnie, I know this is risky, but could you get Gertrude to kneel? Tangi won't be able to jump up that high. Nor me.'

Bonnie says, 'Hoosta.' Gertrude groans as she goes down.

Alex picks up Tangi and hands her to Bonnie. 'Good girl, Tangi,' Alex says. 'I can't hold both you and Summer.' He climbs into the second saddle to take Summer's weight from Bonnie.

They're halfway across the paddock when Sully and Asmaan pace up to them. Summer is listless, lying against Alex, who cradles her in both arms so she won't slip. He's holding the curved bar on the back of Bonnie's saddle with one hand.

'I think she's okay,' he says to Sully's raised eyebrow. 'Broken ankle maybe, scratches. She must have been in the tree half the night. She's exhausted and probably dehydrated.'

It takes an hour to walk back to the truck and lead the camels up the ramp, and they groan all the way. Another ten minutes to the hospital in town. Poor Summer doesn't say a word, and looks white. Alex has never been so glad that the town campaigned a few years ago to keep their little hospital and won.

Sully drives the truck right up to the emergency door and rings for help. They sit in the waiting area while the nurse on duty sees to Summer and calls the local doctor just in case. There is good phone coverage, so Alex calls his mum. 'Can you please call Mrs Holding and let her know we found Summer? We'll leave her here at the hospital. Dr Rana is coming to check her ankle, and Sophie's mum's on duty too and will look after her until Mrs Holding comes.'

Sophie's mum checks out Tangi as well as Summer. 'Tangi's lucky. That wild dog only had her from the back of the neck. Clever dog you have – she must have swivelled. Dogs usually go for the throat.'

On the way home in the truck Alex has his arms full with Tangi. She's worn out like Summer. She tries to lick his hand but misses. 'Your laces are undone. Hey, tooth marks. Looks like these boots might have saved you from a broken leg too.'

'Good thing she was there,' Bonnie says. 'That wild dog might have brought Summer down but for Tangi. She blocked the way to give Gertrude time to get angry.'

Alex wonders if Gertrude was protecting both Tangi and him. Tangi opens her eyes and shuts them again.

'Thank goodness it wasn't a dingo – they can climb trees.'

Alex grins at Bonnie. 'I wonder what Summer thinks about camels now.'

Twenty

||||||||||||||||||||||||||||||||||||||||||||||||||||||||||||||||||||||

On Tuesday, Summer turns up at school in a moon boot, with crutches. Alex can't help admiring her guts. When she sees Alex and Bonnie on the veranda outside their class, she hobbles over. She looks like she hasn't slept for a week. She doesn't even say hi. 'How did you know where to find me? I thought I was going to be dog meat for sure.' She gives a wry grin and Bonnie chuckles.

'That's some pun, Summer.' Then she adds, 'It was Alex.' Summer's gaze switches to him.

It's the first time she's stared at him when he hasn't felt nervous. He shifts his feet. 'I knew what I'd do if I had to move into town after growing up on a property.'

Tears pool in Summer's eyes. She blinks and says, 'But wouldn't a ute be quicker?'

Bonnie answers that. 'Camels can track and find things, similar to dogs, especially ours because they're trained. We could see further on a camel, and besides, some of them can kick feral dogs.' She grins and so does Summer.

'That dog was the scariest thing I've ever seen. A king brown won't go you like that if you leave it alone. That dog had to be starving to act like such a monster. I was sure it would jump high enough to rip my leg off. When I saw you on a camel, I thought I was hallucinating.' Her eyes get misty. 'I couldn't hold on anymore, I was going to die—' She stops suddenly and Bonnie steps forward and hugs her. Summer stands awkwardly with the crutches.

Bonnie moves back. 'We're glad you're okay.'

'Thank you.' Summer bites her bottom lip. 'Um, you having that transmutation thing tomorrow?'

'Yep.'

'Can I come? My father's back from fencing. I can ask if he's interested in helping. He's looking for jobs and I'm sure he'd love one that's helping the school, the community and the environment.'

Bonnie nods. 'Sweet, Summer. Thanks.'

Alex realises he has something to say too. 'I'm sorry, Summer, for thinking you didn't understand about living on the land. I shouldn't have got angry with you.'

All she does is nod, but Alex knows he's forgiven.

On Wednesday morning, Alex tees it up with his mum to bring Dad to school at lunchtime for the Transmutation Project. His dad doesn't seem as interested as he did last week, but when he sees Summer's dad he brightens. 'Joe, g'day.'

'Good to see you, Tom. How are ya?'

Alex stiffens. Has anyone asked his dad that question lately? He and his mum don't dare.

His dad hesitates. 'You know, one foot in front of the other.'

Joe grins. 'Know what you mean, mate.' And he pulls Tom into a man hug. 'Looks like we're working together on this project. Interesting, eh?'

Alex's dad nods. 'Not seen anything like it.' They start talking, Joe mostly, about how they'll work together. Joe will coordinate the project and make a roster for adults to help the children. Benjamin puts his hand up to be on the roster.

Alex likes the way Joe treats his dad, like nothing is wrong, just that he's having a hard time. It reminds Alex of how Roger, Charlie and Sully treat his dad, just accepting him for who he is, not a guy who has depression. A sentence in Kris's Black Dog book comes to Alex: *You have an illness but you are not defined by it, it's only part of you.*

Alex picks up a texta and draws shapes of plastic on a board suitable for a sign: all sorts of bottles, cups, bowls, picnic utensils, ice-cream containers. He writes the words in balloon letters: *Bring your clean plastic here.* The mid-primary kids take the sign to the adjoining art studio to paint the words and shapes. Another group of younger kids decorate the cardboard box the machine came in to go with the sign for the plastic. Bonnie is supervising, with Summer helping from a chair.

By the end of the lunchbreak three bowls are made. Bonnie's pleased. 'Look at all the plastic that went into those bowls. We're going to shred up all the plastic in this whole district.' Some kids clap while Bonnie thanks Joe and Tom for their part in working on the machine.

Sophie bursts in with *The Transcontinental*, the local rag from Port Augusta. 'Look at this!' she cries.

Bonnie rushes over. 'What is it?' Alex looks up.

'You, Alex and Harry and Tom and Roger are in the paper. With the machine.' She looks at Bonnie. 'Have you been in the paper before?'

Alex sees Bonnie hesitate. Maybe she's thinking of the accident when she was eight. That would have been in the paper.

Bonnie glances at Alex and catches his gaze. Then she smiles at Sophie. 'Not for anything good.'

'Well, this is good,' Sophie says. 'You're all famous.'

The bell goes and the kids wash up for afternoon classes. There's a buzz not only in the Transmutation Project Room, but in the whole school. Little kids are talking about transmutation like it's a fun word to use. Alex overhears the Year Fives and Sixes talking about what mould they'd like to get next.

In Alex's classroom, even Tara has forgotten to grimace at Bonnie every time she sees her. She's talking about selling the items. Having a pop-up shop in the library. 'We'll pay off that machine in no time.'

Benjamin is excited to finally have a worthwhile subject for his Year Eleven research project. 'This is decentralising recycling. If all towns could do this, then recycling wouldn't need to be transported great distances or left too long in recycling dumps. With selling back to the host company, I've calculated the machine could be paid off in a year, maybe two for us. Recycling plastics will soon be big business worth billions of dollars to the nation.'

Bonnie listens in amazement. 'He knows a lot about finance.'

'Benjamin is studying economics online,' Alex says.

It all makes Alex grin. For him the best part of the Transmutation Project is seeing the look on his dad's face when the kids said '*Ooooh*' as the first bowl came out of the mould. It gives him an idea.

When he gets home he makes his dad a cuppa. After they've spoken a bit about the Transmutation Project, Alex says, 'I'm making something too.'

His dad holds his gaze. Encouraged, Alex tells him about the sculpture. 'Would you like to see it? I need some help.'

His dad downs the rest of the coffee and stands. He's steadier on his feet and Alex wants to grin, but his eyes tear up instead. By the time they get to the shed where the welder is, Alex has controlled himself.

When he pulls off the old sheet, his dad walks around it, poking and rubbing bits with his fingers. 'You're doing a good job,' his dad finally says. 'This bit here,' he points to where feathers could be, 'you could use lots of fine wire, spread it out like wings.' He looks around at what was once his workshop where he enjoyed making and fixing things. 'I should come down here more often.'

'You could help me do this. It's for Mum's birthday.'

'Where will you put it?'

Alex puts the sheet over the sculpture. 'Let's work out a place now. I was thinking near the herb garden we made.'

'Sounds good.'

Twenty-one

||||||||||||||||||||||||||||||||||||||||||||||||||||||||||||||||||||||||||||||||||||||

Alex calls to Tangi. It's late June and getting cooler. Alex feels the crispness of the air as he surveys the sky with his hands on his hips. There are clouds in the distance, and a kite circling high up or maybe it's an eagle. Dad seems so much better today, and Alex can't wait to tell Bonnie about Dad's interest in Mum's birthday project.

He grins as Tangi bounds up to him. 'You're happy today too, I see.' She barks once. 'Sit. You're always happy.' He puts Tangi's boots on her. 'Your pads must feel better. Bonnie's been a good friend to you.'

Tangi yips and puts out her last paw. Bonnie is certainly what he's needed, too. 'Shall we go to Bonnie's?' Tangi barks and skips around him. 'I guess that's a yes.'

Alex, on Jago, and Tangi, on foot, set off for the camel farm. Alex checks behind him. Tangi is keeping up well. That workout in finding Summer sure helped her get used to those boots. He tries a trot. Tangi trots too for a while, then walks again.

He thinks about Summer. He never thought he'd ever feel positive about Summer. She always seemed prickly, treating him like a kid. But when he saw her stuck in that tree a feeling welled up in him that he had no time to process then. Now he realises Summer isn't an enemy – she may be bossy, but she has her problems too. She doesn't annoy him now and he doesn't need to know if she likes him or Bonnie.

Tangi yips, and it's like a stone falls away inside him – he feels lighter, as if a partition has opened a little. When his dad got sick Alex's heart closed, a bit like the creek full of fallen trees. He may be able to feel compassion for Summer stuck in a tree, bailed up by a feral dog, but can he feel compassion for his dad? He hates that he can even think he might not be able to. All the time he's just wanted his dad back the way he was. But the book Kris lent him says to accept his dad being depressed. Alex wonders how that works.

At Bonnie's house, Alex ties Jago's reins to the tree, leaving a few metres of the rope. Jago only rolls his eyes a bit, like, *Not this again*, and then settles. Next, Alex ties Tangi to the tree.

Bonnie comes over. 'It's working for Jago, hey?'

'Looks like it.'

Bonnie scratches Jago's cheek and he snuffles her hair. 'You're used to Ruby. Now you just have to learn to put up with lots of camels at once.' Alex thinks he wouldn't mind being Jago right then, especially as Jago plants a whiskery lip on Bonnie's face. She laughs. 'He still kisses worse than a camel.'

'That's as close to a kiss as you'll get from Jago.'

She turns to Tangi. 'And you're an energetic girl coming all this way in your boots.' Tangi lifts her chin at Bonnie.

'Tom did well today. Was he okay at home?'

'So far. He's helping me do the sculpture for Mum.'

'That's incredible.'

But Alex knows the illness could still affect his dad even though he has projects to interest him.

'C'mon,' Bonnie says to Alex, 'I want to ask you about the joey.' She leads him to their fenced-in back yard. 'She tried to get over the fence into the paddock yesterday. But she couldn't quite make the jump. I don't want her to hurt herself.' She sighs. 'What do you think, Alex? Is she too young to cope on her own?'

The joey hops over to them and Alex tickles her ears. He thinks for a bit. 'I'd let her live here without being confined and see what happens. Open the gate and she can go into the paddock if she likes or come back. Then she'll decide when she's ready.'

Bonnie nods. 'So, she can stay where water is until she feels safe to go?'

'Mm-hm. Will the camels be okay with her?'

'I've seen them together at Farina. Camels don't bother kangaroos.'

Alex nods.

'Dad said he'd feed her to the eagle.'

Alex is horrified. 'What?'

Bonnie laughs. 'Just joking. Can you imagine Dad killing an animal he didn't have to eat?'

'That's not a good joke.'

'Sorry.' She puts her hand on the gate. 'Dad and Pop said I could decide what to do. I'd like to do it now while you're here.' She speaks as if it's a question, and Alex says, 'Okay.'

'I like the idea of letting her choose.' Bonnie swings the gate open, but the joey doesn't move, just nibbles on the tuffs of dry grass at its feet.

'She mightn't go while we're here,' Alex says. 'Can I see the eagle?'

Bonnie takes some chunks of raw meat out of the fridge in their shed. She brings a thick industrial glove as well. 'Put this on so you can feed Khushi.'

'Khushi?' He raises his eyebrows at her and she beams.

'Pop named her – it means happy. And she does look happier.' Khushi's perched on a branch close to the wire netting, watching Bonnie intently. 'The glove will save your fingers from her sharp beak. Her table manners are appalling.'

This time Alex laughs and Bonnie stares at him. 'That's the first time I've heard you laugh like that, and I wasn't even trying to be funny.'

'Funnier than the last joke.'

He walks along the side of the aviary away from Khushi and stands at the other end. Khushi watches him, her head switching from side to side. She lifts her wings, flaps and flies to him. It's more like gliding, and she lands on a branch close to the wire in front of him.

He pokes the meat through the netting and Khushi stabs at it until it's all gone.

'How amazing being this close to an eagle.' He hopes she can't penetrate the thick glove. Khushi's orange eye comes so close to the wire, he almost flinches. 'She's magnificent.'

Pop hurries over. 'Hello, young fella.'

'Hey. Pity she'll never fly in the wild again.' Alex feels the sadness – like his dad not being able to drive and go where he wants.

Pop says, 'We can let her fly, but whistle her back at first so she doesn't fly too high.'

'What's to stop her never coming back?'

'Food,' Bonnie says. 'Pop's teaching her with a whistle to fly to the other end of the aviary to feed, then we could let her out before a feed and she'll return to be fed.'

'What if she never comes back, though?'

Bonnie shrugs. 'Then she'll be happy even if she doesn't live as long as she would with us.'

Alex stares at Khushi. Maybe doing what you're born to do is better than playing it safe.

'Bonnie's even more happy,' Pop says. 'She keeps talking about a machine at school.'

'It's impressive. We can recycle plastic. And Dad is helping.' Alex hears the sudden pride in his voice – it's so unexpected he tears up. He's been doing that a lot lately.

Pop puts an arm around his shoulders. 'It's good to be interested in life, in living, to love.' Alex wonders if it's Bonnie who's helped Dad with that.

Back home, Alex sits with his phone under the ghost gum to text Lily. Tangi yips, like, *Say hello from me.* She has three boots on. They find the fourth one, and Alex puts it on and takes a photo. He sends it to Lily. She answers straight away.

Cool pic of Tangi. What's on her legs?

Bonnie made boots for her so she can walk further.

Awesome.

We're changing plastic into new stuff at school – called transmutation. Dad's helping.

Sounds exciting. I've got something exciting to share too.

What is it?

Alex wonders if she can surf yet.

I want to study with you next semester.

Alex didn't expect that. His heart beats fast as he keys.

But you chose to live with Nan and Grandad.

I didn't say why. I couldn't cope with Dad's illness, so I basically ran away. Not proud of myself.

She adds a sad emoji.

It's a lot to take in.

Glad you're coming home. Dad will be happy.

Tell him I'll be there soon. Love ya.

Inside, Alex plugs in his phone to charge. Good thing they weren't video-calling – not that the satellite dish would allow that. He smiles to himself as he remembers Lily's words. It's been hard to be left living with Dad's illness. If she were here, she'd be jollying him up like Bonnie does. But would she? How much has Lily changed? Will their family ever be the same again?

Twenty-two

‖‖‖

It's nearly the end of second term and Alex pulls on his jacket. Even though it's winter it's not as cold during the day as it is down south. At assembly, Mr Wanganeen congratulates the students on the Transmutation Project. 'It's great to see you all having this vision of a recycling project to help the environment. This is an encouragement to our whole community during the drought. Now Roger from the Men's Shed would like to have a word.'

Roger grins at them all. 'As you kids probably know, the Men's Shed is where guys get together to create things, fix things. Now we're restoring an FJ Holden. Tom Bray who has set up the transmutation machine will start helping with that.'

Alex sits up straighter. Did he hear that right? Has Roger finally got his dad to go to the Men's Shed? Dad hasn't mentioned it at home.

Roger adds, 'At the Men's Shed we support each other through tough times and raise funds to help the community. We're excited by what you kids have achieved with the Transmutation Project and we want to assist you in it. We'd like to make new moulds for the machine.'

Sophie's mum speaks then. She's on the Governing Council. 'We also are very happy with this initiative and we have decided to order two more moulds from the supplier.' The kids get noisy and Harry adds to it with a galah call.

Mr Wanganeen stands while the kids are still clapping. 'There has also been interest in the Transmutation Project further afield. Our closest sister school would like to send their Year Sevens to see the machine working.'

All the kids clap at this. They only see the kids at this school during yearly swimming carnivals, sports days or weekend sport, since it's forty-five minutes away. 'The visit will happen next Wednesday during our last week of term, and we'll use the occasion to formally launch the Transmutation Project.'

It's mind-boggling, and gives Alex, Bonnie and Harry lots to think about. At lunch Alex makes a new poster for the library. He prints *The Transmutation Project* at the top, then the name of their area school. Underneath: *Proudly supported by SRC, Governing Council, Parents and Friends, Men's Shed.* He adds the General Store, since they said they would sell transmuted items.

'I can't believe all this is happening,' Bonnie says. 'It's like a snowball rolling down a mountain.'

Alex raises his eyebrows. 'You seen snow?'

'Nup. But Mum used to talk about it a lot. Snowballs on mountains was her favourite metaphor.' Bonnie smiles and Alex can see why Bonnie used the present tense for her mum. The past tense sounds so final. 'Let's talk about the school visit this arvo at my place,' she says. 'Then we'll have a plan to share with the kids this Wednesday. There'll be a week after that to get ready.'

Bonnie makes a fuss of Tangi in her boots again when Alex arrives at her place. 'You're a talented girl.'

Ruby is closer than usual, yet Jago doesn't mind. Alex pats him. 'You're doing so much better than a few months ago.'

Bonnie gets Alex talking. 'How's Lily?'

'Nan and Grandad are bringing her home at the end of term, along with Posie, our mare.'

'I'm looking forward to meeting Lily.'

Alex chuckles. 'Yeah, me too. It feels like she's been gone for ages.' He looks up at Bonnie. 'But now things are looking up with Dad getting interested in projects again. You helped with that.'

She smiles. 'And you're okay?'

'Yeah. I just have memories of Lily a lot; Dad too.'

'Can you tell me about them?'

He nods slowly. 'Us camping altogether with Dad, Lil and I riding together, watching the stars near the ghost gum. That was like touching the sky from the heart.' He swallows a lump in his throat. He would never have thought of the sky like that without Bonnie and Pop.

'You'll be able to do all those things again.' Bonnie squeezes his hand.

'Is the joey here?'

Bonnie shakes her head. 'She only comes to have a drink or eat our grass around the house.' She doesn't look too sad about it. 'It's good she can fend for herself.'

Alex nods.

Bonnie has a notebook and she writes all the things they need the kids to do for the school visit. 'Okay, you, Harry and me will show them around.'

'I think Sophie should too,' Alex says.

'Yep. Then lunch. Then go to the Transmutation Project Room. Representatives from all the supporting groups will be there. Can Tom come?'

'I think he'd want to. He's enjoyed everything to do with transmutation so far. We can ask Roger too, as a rep from the Men's Shed.'

'Parents and Friends will do the lunch, so we don't need to bring food.' Bonnie taps the pen against her head. 'Can you think of anything else?'

'Put the box for recycling and posters by the machine, so the visiting kids get all the information they need at once. And copies of the pamphlet about the three-in-one recycle-machine.'

Bonnie writes. 'Good idea.'

Pop comes out of the house with a water bottle and sees them. 'Hello, you two.'

Alex stands up. 'Has Khushi been fed yet?'

'Nup. It's time to let her fly.'

Bonnie's face sparkles. 'Really?'

Alex isn't sure what to think. What if she doesn't come back?

They walk to the aviary. Pop opens the door and Khushi flies to his arm. He strokes her wings and talks softly to her. She pecks around his ear gently.

'That's beautiful,' Alex whispers.

Pop unwinds the string around her foot and throws his arm up into the air. For a nano-second she's suspended, then she flaps, and suddenly she's soaring. Up above their heads, higher than any of the trees. She glides off to the east.

Alex's eyes sting. How good to see her fly high, unencumbered. He wants his dad to soar like that. It's when Khushi banks up and turns to fly north that he feels the uncoiling inside himself. Maybe it's hope. Hope that his dad will get better. A space inside him stretches to love his dad as he is right now.

Pop puts an arm around his shoulders. 'Nature is good at healing itself – it's us that need the help.' Alex nods. Then Pop quotes a line from a poem, about the desert of the heart being where healing starts. It feels like he's saying it especially for Alex and his dad.

They wait together watching the sky as Pop blows the whistle but no black dot reappears.

'I have to go,' Alex finally says to Bonnie.

She can't hide what she's feeling and Alex repeats her own words back to her. 'Khushi's happy doing what she's born to do.'

He puts an arm around her like Pop did to him. She rests her head near his shoulder. 'You're a great friend, Alex.'

189

In his room Alex thinks about what Pop said. It was a lot like a page in the Black Dog book: *The more you hold on to something the more it defines you.* Writing about it, talking about it, helps the healing. Alex draws a picture of his dad on the quad bike with Tangi. Then he writes five things he's grateful for about his dad.

You're strong and are helping yourself to get better. You like teaching kids to do things, first Lily and me and now the kids at school. You talk to me like I matter. You helped me make a herb garden for Mum and now the sculpture. You saved Tangi.

He knows some of these things his dad hasn't done lately, but his dad is still his dad. He is the same person now as the one who taught Alex to drive even though at the moment he's not allowed to drive himself.

Alex thinks of some more things that are different now but don't define his dad. His dad is the same person as the one who took him camping in the Flinders. His dad is the same person who used to ruffle his hair and squeeze him in a man hug. He is the same person who taught him about the stars and how to touch the sky.

Twenty-three

||||||||||||||||||||||||||||||||||||||||||||||||||||||||||||||||||||||||||||||||||||||

Finally, the morning of the school visit arrives. Alex is up early getting all his jobs done. Then he helps with breakfast. His dad is at the table, but he's too quiet. Alex raises his eyebrows at his mum, but she just shrugs. She looks hollow-eyed and it's not even seven yet.

'Did you have a good sleep, Dad?' His mum closes her eyes. Okay, wrong thing to ask. 'Did you have a bad dream?' His father still doesn't answer. It's like they've travelled back in time to a month ago. What could have triggered it this time? There have been no gunshots, dead sheep or high winds.

His dad gets up suddenly and walks out to the veranda. Alex follows him even though his mum is shaking her head. But Kris's book says to encourage the depressed person to talk, to learn about it together and listen.

'Dad, can you say what's wrong? I'd really like you to come to school today to show the visiting kids the machine.'

'I can't.'

Alex knows he shouldn't push, but he can't stop himself. 'Why not?'

'Because I'm not good enough.'

'That's not true. You're my dad and I love you. I think you're good enough.' With relief Alex realises he means it.

'I lost the sheep. It was my fault. Something might happen with the machine too. Those kids might get hurt.'

'Those kids are counting on you, Dad. They love you too.' He hopes that's not putting pressure on his dad.

'The sheep dying was my fault.'

'The drought isn't your fault, Dad. Nor the bushfire. Those things are out of our control.'

His dad turns to him. 'You don't realise – *I moved the sheep.*' He says it slowly, word by word, and Alex stares at him. He didn't know that.

'If I hadn't moved them they would still be alive – we'd have got more for the wool – your mum wouldn't be working in the pub—'

Alex realises what he can say. 'Dad, if they had stayed where they were before you moved them, with the way the bushfire was coming, they would have all been burned. You did the right thing.'

'But over half of them died. We would have lost the lot if not for Tangi. I'm a hopeless farmer making such a crucial mistake and losing so many sheep.'

'Can you control the wind, Dad?'

'Of course not.'

'Don't you remember? The fire was heading straight

for those paddocks, so you moved the sheep. And then the wind changed. Too fast. There was no time to move them back.'

'The wind changed?'

Just then Roger turns up. 'You two having a chinwag?'

Alex nods in relief. Maybe Dad will believe Roger. His place was in the line of the same fire. 'Roger,' he says carefully, 'Dad doesn't remember about the wind changing when we had the fire last year. Can you speak to that?'

Roger starts right in as if he's heard some of the conversation already. 'Yup, you did the right thing, mate. That bloody fire raced all over the place like a cut snake.' He stops. 'Tom, you did the only thing you could. You blocked it out, mate, because you didn't want to remember. Even if you had made a mistake, at a time of crisis like that no one would blame you.'

'*I* blame me. I feel so ashamed – I'm a farmer. A farmer doesn't lose his sheep. He finds them.'

'It's misdirected, mate, believe me. There's no point making yourself miserable like this.'

Dad looks up. 'The wind changed?'

'Like the bugger it was, that fire changed direction many times. I lost sheep too, you know that. The fire was there before I knew it, like a giant blowtorch. I couldn't do a thing. But you did, mate – you tried to save your sheep.'

Alex can see something breaking in his dad. His eyes water, he gulps and Roger puts a hand on his shoulder. Alex goes to his mum and they watch from the window, their arms around each other. Maybe this time it will be a good break for his dad, a break from shame.

At school, Alex does everything they'd decided to do for the visit but he can't help thinking about his dad. He has no idea if he will feel well enough to come. He tells Bonnie.

'Your dad's wellbeing is more important than the machine, Alex. Joe will be there, and Benjamin.'

'I don't want to let you down.'

She actually laughs. 'You wouldn't be able to let me down if you tried, Alex Bray.' Bonnie can be very surprising.

At recess twelve kids, eight boys and four girls, arrive in a minibus with a teacher who drove it. They have self-made name badges that have been created from recycled materials. Bonnie grins at them and they all introduce themselves. Alex recognises some of the boys from footy matches. Not that he's managed to play any this year due to helping at home.

As planned, Alex, Bonnie, Harry and Sophie are the hosts to show them around and then to take them to the staffroom where lunch is served. The Parents and Friends group have brought sandwiches, slices and fruit.

'We can't wait to see the machine working,' Troy, one of the visitors, says.

'Yeah,' a girl called Amber joins in. 'We've learned tonnes of stuff in STEM, but I don't want to read about other people doing it anymore. I want to do it too.'

'I know what you mean,' Bonnie says. 'We felt like that.'

'Sure did,' Harry says. So far he hasn't done any bird calls.

The official launch is set to start at twelve-thirty, and Alex, Bonnie, Harry and Sophie take the guests to the Transmutation Project Room. Some parents are standing in the art studio and watch from there. The kids get settled on the carpet as more parents file in. The mayor of Flinders Ranges district council arrives with Mr Wanganeen. She's well-dressed and wearing high heels. It makes Alex feel their little school is important. Then Joe, and Roger. Alex's heart sinks. His dad's not with them.

'There's my old man,' Harry whispers to Alex. Sure enough, Charlie's at the back, large as life, saying hello to everyone.

Just as Mr Wanganeen moves to the front, Bonnie digs Alex in the ribs. 'Look behind you.' He sees his mum and dad sitting down next to Charlie. What a relief! Alex waves. Kris is with them and gives him a thumbs up.

A journalist arrives with a video camera.

Alex's dad isn't up to speaking in public yet, so Joe Holding explains how the project helps the community and how the Year Sevens have piloted it. Then Joe and Tom show everyone how the machine works. His dad looks lighter; his eyes have a sparkle that Alex hasn't seen for a long time. He is so proud of his dad he has to swallow a lump in his throat.

Alex, Bonnie and Harry have turns putting the plastic in the shredder while Joe and Tom supervise as the shredded flakes are poured into the mould and the other mould is forced on top to create the bowl.

They also show how a doorknob and a comb are made. They're quicker than the bowls. Alex thought it would be ages before they would be able to have different moulds. Now with the help of the Governing Council they will be able to make a variety of things. The camera is making a record of every stage of the process.

Mr Wanganeen returns to the mic. 'Now I would like to invite our mayor to launch the Transmutation Project.'

The mayor's speech is short and enthusiastic. She even makes the kids laugh. Photos are taken with her and the Year Sevens. When the formal proceedings are over, the journalist asks Alex, Bonnie and Harry if they'd answer a question. Mr Wanganeen nods at them.

'Please stand near the machine,' the journalist says. She asks Bonnie first what makes her want to upcycle.

Bonnie starts off like a rocket. 'Too much plastic ends up as landfill and we need to upcycle to stop making more plastic. Did you know that the carbon footprint of one water bottle is eighty-three grams? Did you know recycling one plastic bottle saves enough energy to power a computer for twenty-five minutes? Let's help stop the damage plastic makes to our environment.' Bonnie is impressive.

Alex is next. He's not so good at answering questions on the spot, but he remembers how he felt watching the movie *The Boy who Harnessed the Wind*. 'I want to make a difference, not only for the natural environment but for our district. The drought's been tough for everyone and it's good to have a positive project that will help the area and get everyone involved.'

When Harry is asked the question, Alex thinks he will tell a joke but he doesn't. 'My family is teaching me the old ways of looking after country the way we've always done, before there was manufacturing, cars and plastic, and before coal and oil was dug up. Every little thing we can do helps right the balance in our environment. This is our country together now, so please listen and help us to keep it healthy like it was in the beginning.'

The camera stops. 'Thank you,' the journalist says.

Alex gazes at Harry in amazement. Harry grins. 'Not bad for a couple of galahs, hey?'

At dinner that evening Alex's dad seems more aware than usual. He lifts his head up often and keeps eye contact with Alex.

'It was great at school today. So glad you could come,' Alex says to them both.

His dad nods. 'Thanks for inviting me.' It seems such a usual thing to say, yet Alex senses the meaning behind it. 'You're welcome,' he says in the same tone as his dad. He feels that warm connection with him again.

'Lily will be home next week,' Mum says. 'Nan and Grandad will bring her after the weekend.

'Lily.' Dad smiles. 'Posie too?'

'Yes, they'll bring the float back.' She squeezes Dad's hand. 'It will be like old times again.'

'Our whole family together,' Dad says.

After everything's cleaned up and the dishwasher's on, his dad goes to bed. Alex and his mum sit in the lounge room and do what they haven't done for a year. The talk about Lily coming home starts it. Mum loves looking at photos, so Alex scrolls through his photo folder. 'Look at this.' He shoves it under his mum's gaze as she starts to crochet a square, another thing she hasn't done for ages. It's a pic of his dad on the quad bike, a lamb in front of him, Tangi on the back. He's looking away, at the other sheep probably.

He finds another. 'See? Here's one of Dad holding Tangi. Amazing how he found her last year.'

Alex falls quiet – he remembers his dad's uncontrollable sobbing. It frightened him. That thought startles him. He's never considered that before. His dad was strong; as a young boy Alex thought him invincible. His dad's crying pulled the rug out from under his feet and the world wasn't so safe anymore.

Alex finds another one further back. 'This was on your birthday, Mum, when Dad bought Posie for you.' Alex stares at the photo of his mum on Posie, laughing. His dad is looking up at her with such love in his gaze. It hits Alex afresh: his dad loved them. He still does, even though he can't always show it. He glances at his mum. Her eyes are bleary.

Even if Dad doesn't become totally better, Alex knows they are going to be okay.

Twenty-four

‖‖‖

Friday is Mum's birthday, so Alex has arranged for Bonnie to come over for afternoon tea after school. On Thursday afternoon Alex takes his dad to their shed and they make the last touches to the sculpture.

They've already worked out where to put it by the herb garden. It looks more like a kangaroo now, even though its back is like a dragon's with the ploughshares, and it has wire feathers on its head like Jago's mane. He's made a steel curved tail which keeps the sculpture balanced on the ground. With all the different rusty steel he's used it looks almost steampunk. The focus is the tractor seat in the middle, the very same seat from the old tractor Mum's grandfather used to drive.

'Let's put it there now.' Alex knows it can still be difficult for his dad to wake early.

'Righto,' his dad says. 'You get the dolly.'

Alex drapes an old sheet over the sculpture and positions it on the dolly cart his dad used to move gas bottles or furniture with, then they wheel it to the garden and stop under the gum tree between the herb garden and windmill.

'Dad, can we sit on the veranda? I've got something for you too.'

'Okey-doke.' It's encouraging to hear Dad using phrases he used before he became unwell.

Alex takes out the piece of paper with five things he admires about his dad. He hands it to him.

'You drew the picture of me and Tangi too?' Alex nods. 'You were always drawing as a kid. Glad you haven't stopped.'

'Thanks, Dad.' Alex watches his dad read it, sees him smile and then look sad. 'What's wrong?'

'I'm sorry I got sick.'

'You couldn't help that, Dad. I understand now. It's an illness, not a weakness, and you are the same person now as you were a year ago. I love you, Dad.'

His dad hugs him for a long time.

That night Alex finishes his mum's card. He has written all the things he loves about her and is thankful for even if she's too tired to show them. Then he draws a picture of Tangi sitting on a stump watching over the property.

In the morning after breakfast, Alex and his dad lead Mum blindfolded to the herb garden.

'Can I look now?'

Alex whips the sheet off the sculpture. 'Yeah, happy birthday, Mum.'

She removes the tea towel. 'What's this?'

'Your birthday present. Dad helped.'

'Ohh – Alexander. You both did this?' She touches a ploughshare, a piece of chain, a rusty spanner, puts a finger on a blue willow crockery eye.

'Mm-hm.'

She glances at them in turn. 'You're good at keeping a secret. It's beautiful, Alexander. I had no idea you had this talent.' She's almost in tears, and his dad moves closer. 'Alexander, you are a wonderful son. So like your dad.' She sniffs and grins at Tom.

'You can sit in it.' Alex turns her around and she dutifully sits.

'It's more comfortable than it looks.' She gives a short laugh.

He hands her the card. 'You can read this later when you're having a coffee on this seat.'

'Thank you.' She puts it in her pocket.

He and his dad put their arms around her in a group hug. 'Let's have breakfast,' Alex says. 'I'll cook scrambled eggs.'

During breakfast Charlie drops *The Advertiser* in. 'Thought you might like to see this. Should cheer you up.'

They've made the front page of the regional section. It has a similar title as the local paper: *Students Change Their World*.

There's a text from Lily. Alex can imagine her squealing.

I saw you in the Advertiser! Dad too! Can't believe it!!!!
Bonnie started it.

But Alex knows he had a part to play too, just like he can have a part in supporting his dad, helping him get better so that like Khushi he can fly again.

Bonnie arrives on Ruby after school and ties her up by the shed where Jago hangs out. 'Happy birthday, Rachael.' She hands Mum a round cake tin. 'Chocolate with coffee crème!'

'Thank you.' Mum's eyes shine as she finds candles. 'We can enjoy that when we talk to Lily in a little while.'

They graze on a cheese platter and muffins that his mum made.

Rachael asks Bonnie, 'Do you have any family birthday customs?'

Bonnie hesitates. 'Pop doesn't do a lot with birthdays, nor Sully really.' The corners of Bonnie's mouth droop, something Alex has never seen.

'You'd better all come here when it's your birthday, then,' Alex's mum says, and Bonnie brightens.

Just then they hear a step on the veranda. 'G'day.'

'Sully.' Alex didn't hear the ute, and Tangi doesn't bark for Sully. Alex lets him in. Tangi goes to him, her tail wagging. 'G'day, Tangi.' He looks up after patting her. 'Evening, Rachael, Tom, Alex.'

'Coffee?' Rachael flicks the switch on the coffee machine.

He nods, smiling. 'I hear Asmaan and Gertrude are still happy here?'

'Yes, thank you,' she says. 'Can we keep them a bit

longer – just in case? Food for feral animals will be even harder to find in winter.'

Sully glances at Tom, who nods at him. Alex sighs. Has his dad changed his mind about camels?

'No worries. You're welcome to them. I popped over because I've had a tip-off. You'd better turn the TV on.'

They move to the lounge room to see what Sully means. ABC North and West from Port Pirie air the news as usual. Then, there on the screen Alex sees his dad helping Freddy's little brother put plastic in the shredder.

The scene switches to Bonnie talking, then himself and Harry. The journalist didn't leave out a word. Alex thought she would only use a little bit, or just show one of them talking. The video intersperses their answers with shots of the machine working, the shredding, the bowl coming out of the mould, but the video ends with Harry's words: *This is our country together now, so please listen and help us to keep it healthy like it was in the beginning.*

The news commentator remarks on how we all can make a difference by listening to our children.

'Incredible,' Bonnie says.

The Zoom call alert warbles soon after. Lily's still excited about the media coverage for their school. Nan and Grandad are watching Bonnie and Sully so curiously, Alex is reminded of Khushi's beady eye staring at him. It's embarrassing, but Bonnie and Sully take it in their stride. They light the candles, sing 'Happy Birthday', and eat the cake in front of his grandparents and Lily while they talk.

'That cake looks delicious,' Lily says. 'Did you make it, Alex?' She sounds dubious.

He shakes his head. 'Bonnie did and it's amazing.'

'Mum used to make this cake,' Bonnie says with a glance at Sully. He squeezes her hand.

Then Nan throws a grenade through the screen – at least, that's what it feels like. 'Alexander, will you be down for school with us next year?'

Bonnie's mouth drops open, and his mum watches him closely. Even his dad turns his head to see what he will say. Alex hasn't even spoken with his parents about it yet. 'Um—' It's now or probably never. He has to nip this in the bud.

'I want to stay here.'

He glances at his mum and dad, and what he has feared all this time doesn't happen. They don't frown or protest. They look happy. It gives him courage and he turns back to the screen. 'Thank you so much for the offer, Nan, but I want to study at the school up here.'

Even Nan doesn't argue like he thought she would. All she says is, 'Well, no doubt you can review it again when you reach senior high.'

Lily says into the pause, 'I'm so excited to see you all soon. We'll come after this weekend. I've started packing already. And I've got my Ls, so I'll be able to drive up.'

Dad's smiling as the Zoom session finishes and Sully stands. 'Thank you for a wonderful evening.'

Outside, Sully attaches Ruby's rope to the ute and drives out to the road with Bonnie waving back at them.

Alex clears the table. 'I'll clean this up in the morning, Mum. Let's sit outside.'

He makes her and his dad a coffee and a hot chocolate for himself. They all sit on the veranda where they can see the remains of the sunset, the stars starting to show in the dark blue above. His mum sighs as she zips up her fleece jacket against the cool of the evening.

'Thank you, Alexander, it's been a lovely day and evening.' They sit quietly awhile, then she says, 'You know, Alexander, the kind words you wrote in my card helped today.' Alex stares at her. 'It pulled me up short. It was like I had been given another mother's card by accident.' She takes it out of her pocket.

'And then I realised, it *is* me. Me before the drought . . . I'm so sorry, Alexander.'

He can see the beginnings of a smile on his dad's face. 'We'll all be together soon when Lily's back.' It's like he's saying, *We'll start again*.

Alex hopes so. His family has been through a lot but maybe now they can just wait the drought out together – for surely one day it will rain.

Author's Note

|||||||||||||||||||||||||||||||||||||||||||||||||||||||||||||||||||||||||||||||||||||

The Flinders Ranges is one of South Australia's most magnificent landscapes. The Adnyamathanha (meaning hills or rock) People are the traditional custodians of this diverse landscape, which is world-renowned for its wealth of natural and cultural significance. It is such a beautiful and special place that many people visit and camp there. This was the first holiday destination my husband introduced me to after our marriage, and I have loved it ever since.

Scientists say the Flinders Ranges is the only place on earth where 350 million years of near-continuous geological sequence can be seen, showing the advance of a habitable planet and the arrival of animal life. You may like to watch the video about the World Heritage Nomination of the Flinders Ranges; it's listed in the 'Find out more about . . .' section at the end of this book.

The Flinders Ranges is situated approximately 380 kilometres north of Adelaide, 85 kilometres north-east of the municipal seat of Quorn and 130 kilometres north-east of the regional centre of Port Augusta. Alex and Bonnie live in the Flinders Ranges area. Even though they are 70 kilometres from the centre of the ranges, Wilpena Pound, they can still see the ranges from Rocky Peak.

Rainfall is erratic in this area. Some years there is almost none; at other times storms dump so much rain that there are floods. South Australia is the driest state in Australia. Four-fifths of the state receives annual rainfall of less than 250mm.

From 2017 to 2022 there was a severe drought in the Flinders Ranges area. Drought is defined as a prolonged, abnormally dry period when there is not enough water for the population's normal needs. Drought is not just low rainfall, or much of inland Australia would be in perpetual drought.

In 2018, I visited Arkaroola in the northern Flinders Ranges. The drought at this time was so severe that not only were yellow-footed wallabies dying, but even snakes and lizards as well. The environment looked so apocalyptic that visitors wept.

Alex's story is set in 2020 when his family has already experienced years of drought. It took another two years for the drought to break with a wet spring. Alex is passionate about making Spring Park more sustainable, as climate change increasingly threatens his family's livelihood on the land.

I have endeavoured to show the difficult climatic and economic conditions on a property during drought, but I also wanted to show the effect drought has on the emotional and mental health of people living on the land. Alex's dad has been having difficulties ever since he had to kill his burned sheep. Even less adversity than this has caused many farmers to become depressed during drought conditions. Alex's farm is a long way from the city where counsellors work, but Alex's dad is able to take advantage of telehealth appointments. With medication and help from his counsellor, family, friends and the community, Alex's dad does make progress towards a healthier future.

Alex is a descendant of Cornish settlers, while Bonnie is of Afghan heritage. Her ancestor came to South Australia in 1865 with the first shipment of 124 camels. The camels were off-loaded at Port Augusta and taken to Beltana, which became a camel station. Pop knows all these stories about his ancestor, Taj Saleh, and tells some of them to Alex. Taj is a fictitious character whose story is told in my 2011 novel *Taj and the Great Camel Trek*, which focuses on the great contribution Afghans and their camels made to outback Australia. People like Bonnie's dad rescue feral camels and train them to become domestic animals. Now camels are used for treks and rides along beaches, as well as providing camel milk, cheese, and meat. Many are shipped to Saudi Arabia. In certain areas of Australia, camels are quickly becoming a favourite paddock pet along with alpacas.

Bonnie is interested in Indigenous plant species as they are hardy and well adapted to the dry environment. They don't need more water than the climate supplies, or more fertiliser than the soils contain, and no pesticides are required as they're adapted to Australian pests. These plants are sustainable, with large root masses, and they sequester carbon; that is, they capture carbon dioxide before it enters the atmosphere to contribute to climate change. Bruce Pascoe, author of *Dark Emu*, believes if we dedicated 5 per cent of our current farming lands to these plants, we'd go a long way to meeting our carbon emission targets.

Rosanne's experience of drought

I was born in Penola, South Australia, and spent my earliest years on a sheep farm. When I was six years old, my family moved to Central Queensland. There I grew up near a tiny town called Banana, on a mixed-farming property during a long drought. I attended a one-teacher school for my primary school years. To get to school I would travel for almost an hour on a converted cattle truck, which picked up students from all the properties along the way. A few children lived in the township of Banana, and they could walk to school. My older sister went to boarding school as there was no high school in the area.

On Saturdays, I was given the job of watering a small rose garden with bore water. I had to hold the hose at all times. But I liked to read, and when turning pages I needed to put the hose down or they'd get wet. One day my brother caught me not holding the hose, and I was in big trouble – no one was allowed to waste water. As the youngest, I was always last in the bath, and my mother washed my hair only once a week. On Sunday I wore my hair in a ponytail, but by Friday it was in plaits so no one could see it was dirty. Showers were not permitted, and I was never allowed to let the tap run – I washed my hands in a bowl.

My parents often had quiet conversations that I couldn't hear well, but I knew they looked worried. Words like 'drought', 'bank', 'loan', 'debt' and 'sell up' filtered through.

When I wasn't at school or on the bus run (which took up considerable time), I walked long distances on the property with my kelpie-cross dog, Teddy, climbed the windmill to draw and sometimes rode a horse. I saw the sea once a year. I never wore a raincoat or used an umbrella. Most importantly, I learned never to waste water and even now cannot bear a dripping tap.

Acknowledgements

||||||||||||||||||||||||||||||||||||||||||||||||||||||||||||||||||||||||||||||

As usual, it takes a community to create a novel. I wish to thank all those who were part of my 'community' while I was writing *Alex*. I'm so thankful for the following people who have helped with research, ideas, photos and information: Bradley and Natalie Scott from Transmutation, Robe, South Australia (transmutation.com.au), Ailsa Green, Allen Kelly, Adrian Laubsch, Heidi Laubsch, Pam Williams for Lanky, Tim Prior, Sam Prior, Roger Jaeger and Hayden Kupko for sharing your research on saltbush.

I would also like to acknowledge Nick Pezzaniti, Carolyn Slade for dog-boot information, Gary Schmidt and Rebecca and Frank Lyman for your hospitality. Thanks to all those who gave me fresh insights into sheep farming and other aspects of the novel, and Ro Olafsen and my Kapunda writing group who prayed and egged me on. I am very grateful to my family and especially my love, who cooked so I could meet deadlines.

Thank you to those who have read drafts, especially Michael Hawke, Allen Kelly, Ailsa Green (twice) and Dearne Prior, and for your excellent suggestions. Any mistakes in the text about sheep farming, transmuting plastic, saltbush, or any other aspects of the novel based on the research that was shared with me, are my mistakes only.

Most of all, this novel would not be what it is today without the excellent advice I received from series editor Lyn White. Also, many thanks to Hilary Reynolds, Jodie Webster and the Allen & Unwin team for your tender care of Alex's story.

The line on page 38, 'Only from the heart can you touch the sky', is from the Persian poet Rumi.

The line Pop refers to on page 189, 'In the deserts of the heart let the healing fountain start', is from W.H. Auden's poem 'In Memory of W.B. Yeats'.

The picture of Tangi on a stump that Alex draws was inspired by a Christmas card by Jayden McClymont, given to me by Rebecca.

Timeline

2017–2019

The Australian Bureau of Meteorology (BOM) declares the three years from January 2017 to December 2019 the driest on record for any 36-month period. This record includes the average rainfall totals for the Murray-Darling Basin and New South Wales.

2019 April

The BOM reports large parts of South Australia (SA), New South Wales and the Northern Territory have recorded between 0 and 5 mm of rainfall this month.

June

A study by the University of South Australia shows droughts are becoming longer and more severe in SA with long-term reductions in rainfall.

2020 November–January

Extended heatwave conditions combine with the dry landscape and strong winds to create unprecedented fire weather conditions. Devastating bushfires rage throughout SA, destroying many areas of the state with 278 838 hectares burnt and 67 928 livestock lost.

2020 7 October

Torrential rain falls in in many towns in SA. Hawker receives 32 mm of rain in just 24 hours – more than its monthly average in a day. Tourists are stranded as SA is drenched in much-needed rain. Flash flooding occurs, but within days the creeks dry up again and weeks later the dust storms return.

2022 June–October

Drought conditions ease as SA experiences an unusually wet winter that continues into spring, producing the wettest October since 1900. The Flinders Ranges area has its wettest October on record with more than 100 mm of rain.

Find out more about . . .

Drought
kids.kiddle.co/Drought

youtube.com
Search for 'Drought in Australia – Behind the News'

Flinders Ranges
youtube.com
Search for 'Flinders Ranges – drought, dust then flooding rains'

environment.sa.gov.au/topics
Search for 'Flinder Ranges World Heritage nomination'

history.flindersranges.com.au

South Australian Farmers and Drought
youtube.com
Search for 'Drought threat becomes reality for South Australian farmers'

youtube.com
Search for 'SA Hub snapshot: South Australian Drought Resilience Adoption and Innovation Hub'

Hawker, South Australia
aussietowns.com.au/town/hawker-sa

hawkervic.info

Transmutation
kidsinadelaide.com.au
Search for 'Transmutation Robe – Reduce, Reuse,
Recycle'

transmutation.com.au

Camels in Australia
abc.net.au
Search for 'Pet Camels'

kids.kiddle.co
Search for 'Australian feral camel Facts for Kids'

Culling
news.com.au
Search for 'Indigenous leaders give go-ahead
for massive cull of 10 000 feral camels in remote
South Australia'

Literature
Hawke, Rosanne. *Taj and the Great Camel Trek*,
University of Queensland Press, 2011

French, Jackie. *The Camel Who Crossed Australia*, Harper Collins, NSW, 2008

Johnstone, Matthew and Ainsley. *Living With a Black Dog: how to take care of someone with depression while looking after yourself*, Pan Macmillan, NSW, 2008

Mumu Mike Williams. *Kulinmaya! Keep listening, everybody!* Allen & Unwin, NSW, 2019

Pascoe, Bruce. *Dark Emu*, Magabala Books, Western Australia, 2014

Pascoe, Bruce. *Young Dark Emu*, Magabala Books, Western Australia, 2014

Thunberg, Greta. *No one is too small to make a difference*, Penguin Books, New York, 2020

Wilkinson, Carol. *Atmospheric: The Burning Story of Climate Change*, Walker Books, NSW, 2015

Mental Health Support

farmsafe.org.au
kidshelpline.com.au
headspace.com
beyondblue.org.au

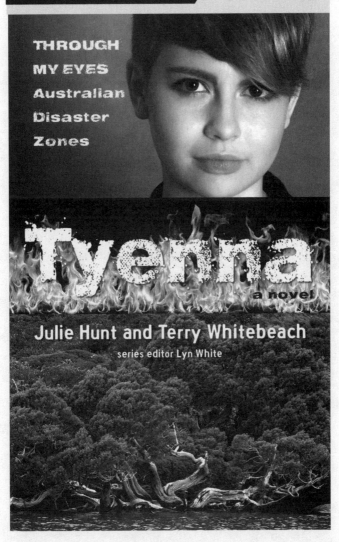

THROUGH MY EYES   OUT NOW

THROUGH MY EYES
Australian
Disaster
Zones

Mia

a novel

Dianne Wolfer

series editor Lyn White

A powerful story of one girl's experience of
2019's Cyclone Veronica in Western Australia

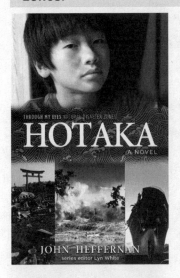
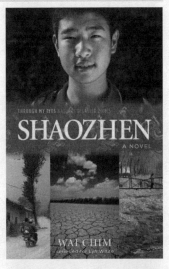

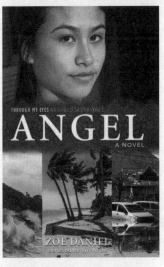